MW00324954

DR POTTER'S PRIVATE PRACTICE

A CHRISTMAS MYSTERY FOR VITA CAREW

FRAN SMITH

HOG FEN
PUBLISHING

Copyright © 2021 by Fran Smith
All rights reserved.
No part of this book may be reproduced in any form or by any electronic or
mechanical means, including information storage and retrieval systems,
audio or video format, without written permission from the author, except
for the use of brief quotations in a book review.

❀ Created with Vellum

CHAPTER 1

EARLY DECEMBER

*C*omfortable in the butler's pantry, Litcombe was enjoying the newspaper with his feet on the fender.

The housekeeper knocked gently and put her head round the door. 'Lady Celia's with that Doctor Potter again, Harry. Will you carry up the tea? We can all smell the drink on him. You know what he's like, whispering and leering, free with his hands. I had three of the maids in floods of tears last time. It's easier if you take the tray up.'

Litcombe sighed and flicked his paper to fold it. 'Where to?'

'The yellow sitting room, by the small fireplace. The tray's all ready.'

'Staggering drunk by two in the afternoon and grabbing every maid he passes,' Litcombe remarked, as he reached for his jacket, 'fine sort of a doctor that one is.'

'Just one or two small matters, Doctor,' Lady Celia said.

Potter nodded, glancing away along the familiar length of

the country house's vast sitting room. Lady Celia always gave him tea here, at the very end, by the smallest fire. What sort of doctor, he wondered, would merit the grand central fireplace, the finest furniture, the very best tea cups? A Fellow of the Royal College of Surgeons? One who had delivered a royal baby or two, perhaps? Certainly not a humble practitioner who had been at the family's beck and call for twenty years.

Lady Celia observed him in her turn as she sipped her tea. The doctor had been a handsome enough man once, but his features were blunted and his cheeks florid now. *He has lost his looks*, she thought, *but he still has his uses*.

'I'm told that you occasionally arrange for patients to board in a kind household near your practice. Is that correct?'

'I have made such arrangements occasionally, yes.'

'We have an elderly - that is to say a long-retired - member of the staff here, a former housekeeper, who is in need of a kindly place.'

'She is unwell?'

'She is seventy-six years old.'

'And infirm?'

'No. She is elderly, but hale and hearty.'

'And she lives here, at present?'

'In her old rooms in the servants' quarters. It has become inconvenient. Her rooms are needed. She has a pension and living arrangements settled on her by my late father-in-law. He was extremely generous to the staff in their retirement. Far more generous than we could possibly be now.'

'Indeed.'

She glanced at him to check his tone. He seemed sincere enough, but it was difficult to be sure with Potter.

'My father-in-law was certainly kind-hearted, but he was

perhaps also...' she hunted for the right word, 'a little improvident. One expects a retired housekeeper to...'

Her Ladyship paused as Litcombe re-entered and added hot water to the teapot. 'Thank you, Litcombe. That will be all.' She waited for the butler to leave and close the door before continuing, leaning forward confidingly as she spoke. 'One expects a retired member of staff to live out a comfortable retirement of a few years. Perhaps two years, or three, but *ten*! A decade at our expense. Really, it exceeds all limits!'

Lady Celia's sharp laugh hung in the air.

Potter was not steady on his chair, she noticed. He swayed, as if to a slow internal pendulum.

A silence fell. A dog barked somewhere in the depths of the great house. Coals shifted in the fireplace.

'You would consider offering this person accommodation? Under your own medical supervision?' Lady Celia prompted.

Potter took a sip of his tea. 'There are considerable expenses involved in such arrangements, Your Ladyship,' he said. He leaned to place his cup and saucer on the small table, but misjudged the distance the first time and only managed it with a jerk and rattle the second.

'We would, of course, cover those expenses,' she told him. But then, pausing with her cup held in front of her face, she added, 'within reason.'

Potter raised his eyebrows a fraction and caught her eye.

'Three months?' he asked.

She shook her head - a quick spasm. 'Three weeks,' she said. 'By Christmas at the very latest.'

Potter looked away again, appearing to study the large ancestral portrait above the fireplace. 'Could I not deal with the matter here?' he suggested.

'No.' Lady Celia's answer was curt and definite. 'It must be elsewhere. There have been remarks - nothing too troubling, but nonetheless, it should happen elsewhere.'

'As you wish,' Potter said. 'All other arrangements - the fee and so on - will be as before, I take it?'

Her Ladyship's fingers drummed lightly on the table. 'Promptly on completion, as before,' she agreed.

Potter slapped both hands on his knees in a gesture of finality. 'Then I shall make preparations for your former housekeeper's warm welcome in Halsey.' He made as if to stand, but Lady Celia raised a hand to detain him.

'There is one other matter I must mention, and that is a letter I have received from your practice. Normally, my secretary would deal with correspondence, but it was addressed to me personally. It is signed on your behalf, but you did not sign it with your own hand.'

Potter frowned and coughed, raising a fist to his lips. 'What does it say?'

'You do not know? This Finch person sends correspondence without your knowledge?'

He shrugged. 'Miss Finch is my clerical assistant. I have no recollection of her needing to write. May I see the letter?'

'I do not have it by me.'

'What were its contents?'

'It mentioned an additional fee. A *discretionary payment*. I disliked the term.'

Potter's eyes snapped into focus. A servant's quiet footsteps passed on the other side of the door.

'Was any sum mentioned?' he asked.

'The letter referred only to a discretionary payment and offered an assurance of continued confidentiality. I have to tell you that I heartily disliked its tone, Potter. I have not shown it to anyone. I wished to raise the matter with you directly. You have provided loyal service to me, particularly in my son's final illness. No discretionary payments or additional fees have been mentioned before. I have always settled your fee promptly and in full.'

'Any such letter must have been sent in error. You should disregard it,' Potter told her. He sounded irritated.

'Discretion. Confidentiality. It occurred to me that his letter might imply…'

Potter flicked a hand as if swatting a fly. 'It is a clerical error. No need to concern yourself a moment longer, I assure you.'

'THE HORSE IS SOBER, AT LEAST,' Litcombe said. He was standing in his braces and shirt sleeves by the kitchen window, watching the doctor's carriage depart along the grand avenue of chestnut trees. 'I heard they found Doctor Potter dead drunk in a ditch on the Littleport Road last week.'

'That wouldn't be you spreading idle gossip, now would it?' Cook asked over her shoulder. She was rolling pastry.

'I know the carter from Halsey who found him,' the butler said, 'fellow named Jack Bulman.'

Cook wiped her hands on her apron and turned to stir a pot at the back of the range. 'Potter was a good enough doctor once. The mistress relied on him years ago, when the young master was poorly. That was before your time,' she said.

'Potter's taken on a younger man now. Yorkshireman. Proper doctor, Jack Bulman says.'

'Has he still got that dragon Whatsername working for him?' Cook asked. 'Her with the scar? Bad-tempered woman? Looks like she could chew the head off a live goose?'

She stooped to remove a tray of tarts from the oven and began lifting them one by one onto a cooling rack, shaking her fingers now and then when she felt the burn. The smell of hot jam and buttery pastry rose into the warm kitchen air.

Litcombe turned from the window and sidled towards the cooling rack. 'Edith Finch? She's still there, running the place with a rod of iron.'

Cook sniffed. 'Maybe it's her that's driven him to the drink,' she said.

A bell rang on the wall behind them. Litcombe pulled his jacket off the back of a chair and shrugged it on, flicking dust off a lapel.

'Now who's gossiping?' he said, reaching for a jam tart as he passed.

CHAPTER 2

MID-DECEMBER

$\mathcal{H}$e was nearly always late these days. Miss Finch looked at the clock on her office mantelpiece. A patient in ten minutes and no sign of him. She would have to go up.

The doctor's private sitting room was empty, but he appeared as she entered.

'You no longer knock, Edith?'

She was well-practiced at assessing his changing moods. He was tidily dressed. His colour was normal. One of his good days, she thought.

'I knocked. You did not hear me. You have Mr Cox with his neurasthenia at two.'

Potter was knotting his tie. He turned to the mirror over the fireplace. 'Did you write to Lady Celia on my behalf?' he asked, flicking one end of the black silk over the other.

She turned and looked at him without answering, expressionless.

'Did you?' he repeated.

'There is no time to discuss this. You have a patient.'

7

'To hell with Cox and his neurasthenia. Did you write to Lady Celia asking for a discretionary payment, or not?'

'I did.'

'Are you quite mad?'

'We agreed.'

'We agreed to my retirement. Not to make blatant and clumsy attempts to extort money from my patients.'

They confronted each other across the room, the pattern of the rich Turkey rug leading from one to the other. A stiff wind outside the window shook and rattled the bare branches of a gnarled pear tree.

'There are costly practicalities to be dealt with,' she said, breaking the silence.

'What sort of practicalities could lead you to write to a patient on your own initiative and ask for a discretionary payment? Have you no sense of how she might interpret that? She takes it for blackmail, pure and simple.'

'If we are to complete your retirement, and mine, as planned, before the spring, the expenses are considerable. Even the tickets…'

He was raising his voice. 'Are you opening a private fund? Is that it, Edith? Branching out on your own? Salting a little something of your own away?'

'You could hardly blame me if I did. You are not in control of your own behaviour. I cannot trust your judgement. If we are to make the necessary arrangements, it is I who must make them. All of them.'

'What are all these 'arrangements'? Tickets are all we need. It is not so difficult.'

'No! You have no understanding of all that must be done. We must leave here in perfect good standing. All records must be in order. Only then will we truly be free. If anything arouses suspicion, we will be hunted down.'

'Linn is an infant. He won't know whether records are in order. And none of the special patients is likely to say anything. Why should they?'

'No reason,' she said. 'They have benefited, and so have you. But people have noticed, over the years.'

'People!' Potter finished his tie and spun round. 'For God's sake, let's not start worrying about people. Most of them are nothing but servants with nothing to do but spy and gossip. My conscience is clear. I have done only what was necessary.'

'Your behaviour is beginning to suggest otherwise.' She looked away from him as she said this, flinching a little, in expectation of his anger.

'You mean what, by that?'

'Your habitual drunkenness. You are no longer able to control it.'

'Nonsense!' He roared the word, red-faced.

Miss Finch closed her eyes briefly and took a breath. When she spoke, it was in calming tones. 'We are making these plans so that you can retire and repair your own health. You deserve some peace. We both do. It is time to bring this to an end.'

CHAPTER 3

THURSDAY, DECEMBER 22ND

*I*t was only a short walk to the library, but Vita's hands were so cold when she returned that she couldn't fit her key into the keyhole and had to ring the doorbell with her elbow and shiver on the doormat until the maid, Tabitha, came to her rescue.

By the fire in her aunt's studio, the sudden warmth turned her nose red, steamed her spectacles, and made her fingers swell until they looked like butcher's sausages.

'Do they not have a fire in the library, dear?' asked her aunt, who wore fingerless gloves and a woollen scarf as she painted.

'Certainly not,' Vita said, 'think of the fire risk. All we can do is to wrap up warmly and choose our books fast. That's why I went so early, I was on the doorstep when they opened to avoid standing in a freezing cold queue.' She sipped the hot chocolate Tabitha had brought her and coughed.

'And what plans for the vacation, Vita?' asked her aunt.

'Physics mostly, but chemistry and maths too. I really have an enormous amount of work to catch up with.'

Her aunt was finishing one of her portraits of a college gentleman. Louisa Brocklehurst's paintings of such grandees were in high demand, mostly because she had a way of making them appear learned, venerable and distinguished without seeming too aloof or self-important. It took great skill. Academic gentlemen never thought of themselves as vain, but all secretly hoped to appear a shade wiser and more dashing in oils than they did in the flesh. This particular gentleman had a beard so luxuriant that it occupied about a third of the canvas. His eyes, as they peered through woolly eyebrows, were small and extremely fierce.

'I'm afraid Professor McGuinness looks like an angry goat, whatever I do with him,' Louisa remarked, stepping back from her work. 'But apart from your studies, Vita? No Christmas invitations? No parties? No social engagements? No concerts?'

Vita coughed again. She ran her hands over the pile of library books on her knee. 'I went to a party at college, Aunt, and a carol concert, remember? Now I must work.'

Her aunt stopped scrutinising the painting and came over, wiping her hands on a paint spattered rag. 'Vita, my dear, you can't work all the time. One needs rest. One must have recreation. Endless work is oppressive to the spirit. You know it is. I see you looking tired and wan, and I worry. You are young. You should be out enjoying yourself with people of your own age.'

'I have Prelim examinations soon, Aunt, and I am horribly behind.'

Her aunt patted Vita's hand. 'Surely I can tempt you away from your desk, for just a little while?'

'What have you in mind?'

'A little Christmas Eve entertainment - just a few friends, some music and a wonderful dinner. Monsieur's food will be irresistible. Do say you will come, Vita! I have already invited your brother and a few of his friends - we shall have dancing!'

'I thought you said a quiet dinner.'

'I said 'little', not 'quiet', Vita. I am not so elderly that I have to have *quiet* dinners all year round. No indeed! Oh, and I took the liberty of ordering an evening dress for you from Miss Pushkin last time I was there. It is in the most sumptuous scarlet taffeta. A Christmas gift, so no arguments.'

Louisa walked back across the studio, lifted the portrait of Professor McGuinness off the easel and propped it against a wall, giving it one more quizzical look before she turned away.

'I truly believe Miss Pushkin is the most talented dressmaker in Cambridge. Her taste is exquisite, but we must keep her name to ourselves. She will put up her prices if all the college ladies rush to her. Now, I'm sorry to send you out again, dear, but would you mind dropping a note to Professor McGuinness into the post? The sooner he sees it, the better. That beard of his will only keep growing. I have added to it twice already.'

Aunt Louisa bustled off, pulling off her painting apron as she went.

Vita stayed huddled over her hot chocolate, thinking only that a scarlet dress would match nothing but her nose at that moment.

CHAPTER 4

'*A*h, Vita! Just the person I was looking for!'

Vita was so muffled in her hat and scarf that she had almost walked past Dr Goodman, her aunt's neighbour. He was carrying a bulging canvas bag over one shoulder. 'May I ask a favour?' he said, falling into step beside her.

'Does it involve parties and dancing?' Vita asked him.

'Not at all,' he said, laughing. 'It is hospital work of an interesting kind.'

'I have so much studying to do.'

'This will be of great clinical interest.'

'Really?' Vita was already curious, despite her intention to study ceaselessly until the Christmas vacation was over.

'I would like you to visit and talk to a strange patient who was brought early in this morning.' The doctor moved the bag to his other shoulder.

'Strange? How is the patient strange?'

'He has no memory. He can't remember his own name, his past life or anything that has happened.'

'Goodness!'

'He was found on a country station platform, cold and wet

and without shoes. He has no idea who he is or how he got there.'

'Poor man. It there a brain injury?'

'It's too early to tell. There are signs of concussion from a blow to the head. The point is, the nurses are too busy to sit with him and we don't know where to find relatives. He needs someone who will stay long enough to keep him company and encourage him to talk. Anything that will help him remember what has happened.'

'You want me to question him?'

'No. Just sit with him and pass the time in conversation and harmless activity - cards or handiwork, anything that will divert him from his predicament. He is alarmed and unsettled, naturally enough.'

'I imagine I can do that.'

'Can you start today?'

'I shall go immediately. I can post this on the way.'

'Excellent. We are very much looking forward to your Aunt's Christmas Eve dinner,' he said. 'No doubt the French chef has ambitious plans.'

'No doubt he has,' said Vita.

'Wild horses wouldn't keep me away! Now, it is my day off, but the patient is easily found. Ward Two, second side room on the left. Tell them I sent you.'

'That looks heavy,' Vita said, indicating the canvas bag.

'It is my latest invention. I believe it will revolutionise the training of junior doctors, at least in one area. When it is finished, that is. I'm taking it now for its mechanism to be examined in an engineering workshop.'

'May I ask what it does?'

'Not yet! But as soon as it's ready, I shall recruit you to put it through its paces. Let me know how you get on with the patient. I shall be at home for most of the day.'

Goodman strode away in the direction of town, with the sack bouncing on his back and the earflaps on his fur hat flapping on either side.

A half-hearted fall of snow had begun. Indecisive flakes drifted in a heavy grey sky as Vita dropped her aunt's note into the red letterbox on the corner of Eden Street and set out for the hospital.

CHAPTER 5

The patient in the side room was sitting up in bed as Vita arrived. He wore grey and white striped hospital-issue pyjamas. His hands were bandaged, as was his forehead. Both eyes were blackened and his face was badly grazed.

On her walk, Vita had wondered how best to introduce herself. It seemed unkind to give her name immediately to someone who couldn't reply by giving his. She had imagined just shaking hands, but now saw that because his were bandaged, that was not possible either.

In the end, all she did was to smile and say hello.

The young man looked at her, troubled. 'Hello,' he said, 'I'm sorry if I should remember you. I can't remember anything at the moment.'

'No, we haven't met,' Vita said. 'Doctor Goodman asked if I could come and talk to you, in case it helped you to remember.'

'Perhaps it will help,' he said, and pointed to a chair. 'I hope it will. Everything is so blank.'

'You remember nothing?'

The young man frowned and looked down at his bandaged hands. 'I remember waking up here. They told me I was in Addenbrooke's Hospital. Everyone is kind, but I cannot answer any questions. It is strange and confusing. I know it is not normal and I fear what it means. Why would someone's memory just leave them?'

'My name is Vita,' she said.

'A nurse?'

'No. I am a student. I'm studying science. My neighbour, Dr Goodman, is one of your doctors. He asked if I would sit with you.'

'I remember Goodman. He's Welsh.'

'He is.'

It pleased him to get this right. He was a young man, perhaps thirty, pale of complexion and freckled, with light brown hair that waved forward over his forehead and a small fair moustache. His pale blue eyes were bloodshot, the lashes around them almost white. He spoke with a slight accent - northern, Vita thought, but she couldn't place it more accurately than that. To judge by his shoulders, he was strong, with the build of a sportsman, and she guessed him to be quite tall. She sat on the hard hospital chair.

'Is it very cold outside?' the patient asked.

'Yes, cold and snowy.'

'I felt terribly cold. I remember that,' he said.

'You mean before you came here?'

'Yes. I don't think I can remember anything else, though. I damaged my hands and feet, but I don't remember how. Perhaps I fell. It's just blank. If I try to remember, there is just nothing there.'

'But you can remember today? The time since you arrived here? Where you are and your doctors' names?'

'Yes. All that feels normal. I have only the feeling - when

17

I think about what happened to me before - I have only the feeling that it must have been something bad that brought me here. That worries me. I might have done something bad myself.'

He passed a bandaged hand over his chin anxiously.

'Shall we play cards?' Vita suggested, taking a pack of playing cards from her bag. It seemed a good idea to distract him from the gloomier possibilities.

'Do I know how to play cards?' The young man asked. He seemed to be questioning himself. Vita handed him the pack, and to the surprise of both of them, he shuffled it. The movement was made awkward by the bandages on his hands, but they left enough of his fingers free to shuffle the pack several times and deal seven cards into two piles on the bedcover.

'That looks like gin rummy,' Vita remarked.

'Yes,' he said, 'gin rummy. I seem to know how to play.' He smiled, picked up his cards and fanned them in front of him. Vita did the same. They began a game.

'Do you live near the hospital?' the young man asked, discarding one from his hand and looking at Vita over his cards.

'Quite near. During the term I live at Newton College, but it is the vacation now, so I am back in town with my aunt.' Vita discarded one of her cards and picked up another.

'And you study science?'

Vita sighed. 'I try to. I am only in my first year of under-graduate study, and I am not finding it easy.'

'Physics,' he said. 'Physics is hard to get a grip on at first.' He made a face at the hand of cards he was holding and discarded one.

'So you know physics?'

'I do, I think. I don't know how, though.'

Vita decided not to react to every new memory too effusively. She would just be a quiet observer of what leaked back into his mind.

'Physics and mathematics are the subjects that cause me the greatest difficulty,'she said.

'I believe I rather enjoy mathematics,' he said. 'But I can't say whether I could I recall any of it in detail.'

'I have a textbook in my bag, if you would care to try,' Vita said.

'Really? Which one?'

Vita pulled a well-worn brown covered volume out of her shoulder bag. He looked at it in wonder.

'I know it. It is…' he closed his eyes for a few seconds…'Atkins! It is Atkins', *Pure Mathematics*! Am I right?'

Opening the front cover, Vita read the title page aloud: '*Pure Mathematics including Arithmetic, Algebra, Geometry and Plane Trigonometry by Edward Atkins, B.Sc. Published in 1874.*'

'1874!' he said. 'Perhaps I know it from school days. May I look at it?' Vita handed him the book, and he laid his cards aside and read a few pages. 'It seems familiar, but I can't remember where from.'

He looked back at his cards, disappointed that the new memory seemed not to lead anywhere.

'Where are you from, Vita?' he asked, changing the subject. He re-arranged the cards in his hand and put three of a kind down on the bed table between them.

'My family is from Devon. You have a northern accent.'

'My family is from Yorkshire,' he said, picking up another card. 'That just came to me. Nothing else, though.'

'You are a long way from home.'

'Yes, but I don't know how I got here.' He put his cards

down, suddenly. 'I will not play any more now. Please excuse me, but these thoughts, these bits of memories, all broken and unconnected, they churn in my head. It's oddly exhausting.'

'Of course.' Vita collected the cards and prepared to leave. The patient lay back on his pillows.

'Would you come again?' he asked, closing his eyes.

'Yes, if you think it helps.'

'It does. Do come again,' he muttered.

Vita stole out of the ward. He was asleep by the time she had crossed the threshold. The whole visit, she thought on the way home, must have lasted less than fifteen minutes.

DR GOODMAN WAS STANDING in the hall of his house with his sleeves rolled up and the powerful smell of glue about him, when Vita stopped by to report on her first visit to the patient. 'They are notoriously exhausting, head injuries,' he said. 'But it sounds like progress. Will you return?'

'Yes, I should like to.'

'Good work. Now, it is my day off, and I must continue my gluing - we are at a critical moment and I dread one of the children getting their hands on...'

The six Goodman children were an energetic and notoriously mischievous lot.

'... William! I said do not touch! The glue is wet, boy!'

Vita turned to leave, but added one more question. 'They found him at a station, you said?'

'Yes. Waterfen. The crossing keeper found him collapsed on the platform when he came on duty in the morning.'

IT WAS PERHAPS thirty steps across Eden Street from the Goodman's house to her aunt's at number 144. As she took the first fifteen of these steps, Vita pulled Edward Atkins' *Pure Mathematics* out of her bag, thinking she would simply work her way through it for the rest of the day. At about step number twenty-five, it occurred to her that she might easily take the short rail trip to Waterfen station and see what it was like. It might help the patient remember something if she could describe the place first-hand. By step twenty-eight, she had rejected the Waterfen idea because it would eat into the time she needed to dedicate to more practice questions in *Pure Mathematics*. At the front door of number 144, she realised that she could take *Pure Mathematics* on the train journey to Waterfen and try some questions on the way, thus achieving both aims. A perfect solution.

She found her aunt in the basement kitchen discussing dinner party menus with Monsieur Picard, her French chef. Monsieur was wearing his little silver spectacles and holding a pencil in his hand as they both leaned over a long list. It seemed a meeting of the highest importance, and a certain tension pervaded the house, so Vita explained her plan quickly and left them to their polite tussle over the choice of wines.

CHAPTER 6

THE WEEK BEFORE, HALSEY

*A*t the doctor's house in Halsey, Miss Finch looked at the clock on her office mantelpiece. A patient waiting and no sign of Potter yet. She would have to go up to his rooms.

She found him sprawling on the sofa, clothed, but barefoot. With a well-trained eye, she could tell he had not slept in those clothes. His colour was normal. If he had taken whisky that morning, he had taken only a moderate amount.

Since the challenge of putting on his socks and shoes had defeated him, she found them and began pulling the socks over his pale feet. He made no resistance.

'I can remember the first time I saw you,' he said, without moving from the prone position. His speech was only slightly slurred. 'It was at church, remember?'

'I remember,' she said, moving on to the second foot and its sock.

'I looked forward to your father's sermons.'

'You did not.'

'They were so much shorter than Markham's. Markham's sermons were enough to turn anyone Quaker. You could hardly hear a word: mumble, mumble, righteous mumble for forty minutes at a time.'

He propped himself up on an elbow and watched her struggle with his left boot as if the limb belonged to someone else. 'Your father's sermons were a crisp ten minutes. Dull as you like, but plain and audible.'

'He understood his congregation,' she said. 'And you were only there to find new patients.'

He threw himself back onto the cushions. 'You were there to take round the collection plate or read the lesson. I heard you read the Book of Judges once: Samson and Delilah.'

She made no reply. She was having difficulty working the boot over the doctor's right heel.

'You read Delilah's story with remarkable zeal, if I recall.'

'You talk a lot of nonsense.'

'It was the collection plate that made me take a keener interest in you, though.'

'I've heard this before.'

She was tightening laces now, pulling at his unco-operating foot, knotting.

'Half a guinea. Quick as a flash.'

She finished tying his lace and dropped the foot. It fell heavily back onto the sofa.

'Tom Curtis is waiting downstairs,' she said.

'Like lightning, it was. Up your sleeve and into your pocket. You were good at it. And I thought, *well, Potter, what have we here? A vicar's daughter with her hand in the collection plate*. I caught your eye, remember that? And you looked straight back. Unflinching. I had seen you; you knew it. Our secret bond.'

'He's waiting.'

Potter lay back and addressed his remarks to the ceiling.

'Tom Curtis's best friend was shot dead beside him at the Siege of Mafeking. He sees it again, in ugly detail, night after night in his dreams. Tom Curtis returned to a country celebrating Mafeking as a great and noble victory. That is what is wrong with Tom Curtis, and there is nothing I can do to make that better.'

'You see Elizabeth Temple at three.'

'Elizabeth Temple chose a bad, bad husband. I can't cure that either.'

He groaned and pushed the idea of his suffering patients away with a loose gesture of one arm.

Miss Finch walked briskly across the room to throw open a large sash window. A blast of bitter winter air swept the room, rattling the door and lashing the curtains. She strode back to the sofa and stood with her hands on her hips in front of the doctor's prone figure, then reached forward, took him by the shoulders, hauled him into a sitting position, and shook him.

'You will get up, and you will see your patients. And tomorrow you will do the same. They pay for these boots and that sofa.'

'I knew you were the one,' he said. He looked up at her. '*That scar-faced woman who steals from her father's church,* I said to myself. *She will add a bit of pepper to life in this flat and godforsaken backwater.* And I was right, by George.'

She turned away, shaking her head.

'He's in your consulting room,' she said.

CHAPTER 7

THURSDAY, DECEMBER 22ND

*V*ita had to ask several times before she found the platform the London train would pull into before continuing to Waterfen, Ely, and beyond. Other travellers huddled in greatcoats, hats, scarves and gloves, the clouds of their breath mingling with the steam of the locomotives. The snow was still uncertain, fluttering down but not settling yet.

Waterfen station, when Vita climbed down from the train there, was a stark contrast to Cambridge. It was in fields. The other passengers who had disembarked darted away through the snow, and Vita was soon alone on the platform, beginning to think the whole idea had been a mistake. There was nobody here, and nothing to be seen. And if Cambridge station had seemed windswept, its exposure was as nothing to the blasts of arctic air here. The little station had no enclosure of any sort. It was a boardwalk raised above a wide and windy expanse of the flattest fen. Anyone who dawdled there on a December day risked frostbite.

Vita's only recourse was to cross to the other platform and wait for the train to carry her back to Cambridge. She turned to do so, but as she did, a figure trotted out of the cottage beside the line and in a practiced set of movements threw the gates back across the railway track, opening the road. Of course! There was a crossing keeper.

'Everything alright, Miss?' he called, seeing her there.

'I was looking for someone who might have seen the gentleman who was found here this morning,' Vita said, hurrying over.

'I found him myself, Miss. Are you acquainted with him?' the man asked. He wore his cap on the back of his head and no overcoat. He even had his sleeves rolled up. A man of unimaginable hardiness.

'I met him in hospital this morning,' Vita said. 'He has lost his memory. I wondered if there was anything I could tell him, any little detail that might help.'

'You saw him in the hospital? How is the gentleman? He was in a proper bad way when we found him. I thought it was all up with him at first. Blue with cold he was.'

A bell rang. The crossing keeper looked at his pocket watch and glanced past Vita up the line. 'That'll be the London train. If you don't mind waiting here, Miss.'

He darted forward and opened the gates for the train one at a time again before climbing nimbly into the signal box beside the line. Vita watched as the distant chain of smoke-blurred lights grew larger until the train hissed loudly to a squealing, jolting stop at the platform on the other side. A few dark figures stepped out and hurried away with their collars raised against the wind and snow. The engine here in the countryside seemed huge - far larger than it would at Cambridge station. There it was a useful human-scale machine; here it seemed a mighty and far less controllable living beast. It shrieked and roared as it pulled away. The very platform trembled under Vita's feet.

The crossing keeper appeared again, jumping down from

the signal box and re-opening the gates to the road. He came back to Vita.

'I am interrupting your work,' she said.

'No. I have nearly sixteen minutes before the fast train.'

'So it was you who found the man?'

'Yes, Miss. Bob Marshall. That's my cottage.' He nodded to the little house, which from that angle seemed so close to the line that you could reach out of a window and touch a carriage. 'I come over to the signal box at my usual time, just after five in the morning, and see something lying there. I thought someone had dropped something - a coat or a bag, at first, but then I saw it was a man. There were some regulars at the station already, and they give me a hand. A lad ran for the doctor. We carried him into the cottage and set him by the fire to warm him. My missus wrapped him in blankets. He was frozen like a block of ice.'

'He didn't say anything?'

'No. He was mumbling a bit, but he couldn't walk or answer a question. One man thought he was drunk, but he didn't seem drunk to me. I seen a few drunks in my time. He didn't smell of it. He was soaking wet and shivering, and his feet and hands were cut and bleeding. His feet were bare. No shoes. They were blue as blue! He was in a terrible state. Doctor Ware's man came – he lives just up the road – and he said we should send him to the hospital, so we telegraphed down the line for the ambulance to meet the train and put him on the first train to Cambridge. He'd have got there by six.'

'But you didn't see how he came to be on the platform?'

Bob Marshall settled the cap on his head. 'It must have happened after midnight. I checked everything then, after the last goods train. There weren't nobody on the platform then.'

'I wonder how he could have got here.'

'He must have been on foot. Nobody comes past my

27

cottage with a horse and cart without I hear it. I sleep light after all these years listening for trains and signals changing.'

'Was there anything you noticed? Anything not as usual? You must have a sharp eye, Mr Marshall.'

Bob Marshall looked gratified at this. 'I have. That goes with the job,' he said. 'The one thing I noticed was that the old drove gate over there was not quite as it should be. I can't say exactly how. Just a bit different.'

Vita looked in the direction he had indicated. She could just make out an overgrown gateway leading off the road after it crossed the railway. 'Where does it go? You called it a drove road.'

'That runs beside the line for half a mile and then it goes off east across the fen. There's drove roads all round here. Rough old back lanes. Muddy. Not much used. Fen farms off to either side. Miles from anywhere. Lonely old places, them drove farms are. Bleak.'

'I might go and look over there,' Vita said.

'You'll get muddy, Miss. Nobody uses them drove tracks now.'

'I'll be careful, don't worry. What are the farms called down that way?'

'Merrily Farm is the nearest, then Holiday Farm.'

'They are cheerful enough names.'

'It's a kind of fen joke, Miss. They are dreadful poor, grim old places.'

VITA LEFT the platform and crossed over the village road to the gate across the overgrown drove lane. It was broken and down on its hinges, too heavy to shift far, but she squeezed through. The track beyond was overgrown and obviously little used. There were no wheel tracks in the mud. Near the gate there were definitely boot prints, as if others looking for information had milled around, but these went no further than a few feet up the lane. Vita followed, stepping carefully on the grass to avoid confusing any prints in the mud.

About thirty feet along the track, round a bend and with the view of the station blocked by a dense blackthorn hedge, she saw what could be the print of a part of a bare human foot in a patch of mud. It was hard to be sure. Further up there was another print, clearer this time, the heel smeared, but all five toes quite distinct. Freezing rain was falling lightly out of a flat slate grey sky. Vita wondered whether this would obliterate the footprint or freeze - and so preserve - it. Uncertain, she sketched it quickly in her pocket notebook. Her feet and fingers were cold and her sketch clumsy, but it was a record of sorts. The sky was darkening. She wondered whether to go back, not being able to make out any farm or building of any sort as far as she could see down the track.

A train passed. It sounded near, but its lights and the billowing steam were thirty yards or more away. The drove road had turned away from the railway across open fenland. She was near people. She could see that train and hear another in the distance, but even so the drove road felt forbiddingly remote. A dog barked sharply across the fields. It was the deep-throated bark of a large animal. Vita shivered. Something caught her eye on the ground a little further along. It was a torn and damp fragment of white paper, tiny and irregular. She picked it up. Looking further, she thought there was another in the mud a few yards on. She found it, another piece of a torn sheet, damp to the point of almost dissolving. She put both pieces into her handkerchief and folded it carefully. Peering along the track, she saw a tiny white dot that might be another piece and hurried on. The pieces continued.

Each was tiny and torn, but they were similar - possibly torn from the same sheet. They were about thirty feet apart and seemed to end at a fork in the track where a crooked and weatherbeaten sign reading 'Merrily Farm' was nailed to the stump of an old ash tree.

The track to the farm, an untidy set of low buildings at least a quarter of a mile from the sign, was rutted and muddy. Vita could see the parallel ruts of a cart's wheels and churned horses' hoofprints. They looked recent. The throaty bark of the dog sounded closer now. The place looked dark and neglected, but a thin plume of smoke rose from a chimney, so it must be inhabited. The look of the place made her pull up her collar and think of hurrying back to the station. The only reason she did not turn away was that her eye was caught by a dot of white across the rough grass of the field to her right. Another of the torn pieces of paper. She looked for movement among the distant buildings. Seeing none, she passed through the entrance to Merrily Farm and made her way with diffi-culty across the uneven field toward the next scrap of white.

The dog barked several times more, louder now. Reaching the paper and stooping to collect it, Vita could see cart tracks which branched off the main track to the farm, where she stood, and led over the uneven field. The tracks over this rough pasture were indistinct, but even so, the parallel lines of cartwheels were clear enough. They ended twenty feet from where she stood. She crept forward, keeping low, and reared back in shock when a dark hole suddenly opened up at her feet. It had no cover or marker, there was just a round brick mouth opening into a black pit. The cart tracks led to it, stopped at its rim, then doubled back.

A shout rang out. It was a man's voice uttering an angry challenge. His dog barked again, but differently now, the tone changing to outright aggression. Vita picked up her skirts and dashed for the gate, hoping her dark coat would be hard for both man and dog to see against the bare hedges. The gloom of the winter's afternoon closed in. By the time she stopped to catch her breath, the barking had receded, then stopped.

She was still out of breath when she returned to the station. Bob Marshall raised an eyebrow at her damp and bedraggled appearance.

'You didn't ought to go too far down there, Miss. Not on your own. They're none too friendly, some of them farmers. I thought I should have to send a search party.'

'When the police came, did they look down the drove road?' Vita asked him.

'They had a look, but they seemed more interested in the road to the village.' The crossing keeper pulled out his pocket watch and consulted the time. 'I must get back to the signal box,' he said. 'You'll need to cross over. I wish there was more I could tell you to help the poor gentleman.'

They both walked over the level crossing towards the platform on the other side. 'How do you know he was a gentleman? He might have been a tramp, or an escaped prisoner, Mr Marshall, but you never seemed to suspect it.'

'Oh no, he was a young gentleman. We could tell by his suit. One of the regular travellers here, John Towney, he works in a gentleman's outfitters. He said straight away it was a good suit. Well made. He was nicely turned out before whatever happened to him. I reckon it must have been something pretty bad. I even wondered if a train had hit him at first. But nobody reported anything on this line.'

Even the passing thought of a train accident made Bob Marshall shudder visibly. 'The only other thing we could think of was that someone had given him a terrible beating, maybe to rob him. He had nothing in his pockets. We looked to see if he had an address or a wallet on him, but his pockets was all empty. Terrible thing it is to think of it happening round here.' He shook his head at the turn the world had taken at Waterfen. 'Anyway, I'm glad he's not too bad. I didn't ask your name, Miss.'

'Vita Carew.'

Thanking the crossing keeper for his help, Vita handed him one of her aunt's calling cards. He tucked it into his waistcoat pocket and hurried back up the steps to the signal box.

CHAPTER 8

*B*ruises were developing around the scratches on the patient's forehead, but in general a healthier colour was returning to his face.

'It is Vita, I think,' he said, a little tentatively as she re-entered his room.

'It is,' she said, 'but you sound doubtful.'

'I doubt my memory now. I used to assume it was in good order, but now I can't be sure. It is uncomfortable, not knowing the story of your own life. It must be in my head somewhere, but I can't find it. Do you have that mathematics book with you?'

Vita produced *Pure Mathematics* from her bag and passed it to him.

'Now here, I have something I can remember easily. Would you mind if I copied out some problems? They would offer a fine distraction.'

'No indeed,' Vita said. 'I will help and perhaps it will improve my very limited mathematical skills.'

They began taking it in turns to copy questions from the book onto a sheet of paper, the patient writing awkwardly with injured and bandaged hands. It was quiet in the small side room. Someone had hung a bunch of holly and a small paper chain over the bed.

'Mathematics is comfortingly true when everything else is vague,' he remarked, frowning in concentration at his writing.

'I went to the station,' Vita said. 'The one where they found you.'

'What did you do that for?' The patient looked surprised and puzzled.

'I thought if I spoke to people there, I might find some little detail that could help you remember.'

'It is very decent of you to go to such trouble,' he said. 'Did you learn anything?'

'The crossing keeper found you, but he couldn't tell how you came to be there. He is a kind man. He sends his best wishes for your recovery. He was afraid you had been hit by a train, or robbed.'

'I shall write a note to thank him,' he broke off and looked out of the window, 'but I'll not be able sign it. I don't know my own name. It's right strange. It feels close, as if my memories are just there, beyond a closed door or round a corner, only I can't reach them. Doctors say it's likely caused by the knock I took to the head.'

Again, he seemed dispirited. Vita felt a pang of sympathy for the awful loneliness of his situation.

'Working out these mathematical problems, and even the action of holding a pencil in your hand, might elicit something,' she suggested.

He turned to her again. 'I have remembered one thing. Just an isolated memory - an image, really.'

'Go on,' Vita said.

'I was trapped somewhere very black and wet. I was extremely cold. The walls were slippery. It seemed deep, but I

34

couldn't tell for sure. There was a smell of earth, of damp, of vegetation. I could feel brick walls on all sides. I suppose it was a pit of some sort, or a well. I was shocked and my wrists hurt. My head even worse. Dizzy. I could barely stand. I can't tell how long I was there. A long time, it seemed.'

The memory made him shudder.

'Does it feel like a recent memory?'

'I think so,' he said. He looked troubled. 'But it might be a nightmare. My thoughts are right muddled and disjointed. I had a working brain once, I am sure of it.'

A nurse bustled in and thrust a thermometer without ceremony under the patient's tongue. She took his wrist and looked at her watch as she measured his pulse. She was as stiff as her starched white apron.

'Don't tire the patient, please,' she said to Vita. 'He needs rest. Rest and quiet above all for head injuries.'

She left as briskly as she had come; her booted footsteps tapping away down the corridor.

The patient looked after her. 'I know a nurse,' he said. 'It's all confused, but I seem to remember a pleasant nurse.'

'Well, I hope the nurse you know is a little less sharp than that one,' Vita said, laughing. 'But perhaps she has a point, and I should leave you to rest.'

He lay back for a moment, closing his eyes, but then sat up again suddenly. 'I climbed out! I remember it. Hours, it took; hours and hours. I kept falling back. The stones scraped my hands. Slippery and narrow, it were. I kept falling. The fall was worse every time, but I could see light. I'd my mind made up. I meant to get out. I weren't going to die in some hole. How long it took, I couldn't rightly say. It were that exhausting, all I could do was lie on't grass, when I got out.'

Reliving the memory brought out his Yorkshire way of speaking. He lifted his bandaged hands and looked at them, rotating them and stretching the fingers. The pain was sharp enough to make him wince.

'And my feet. I remember now, I took my shoes off. It were easier to climb barefoot.'

'That must be how your feet were so damaged,' Vita said.

'I tried putting my shoes in my pockets, so I could walk in them later, but they wouldn't stay. They fell out. I remember hearing them fall one at a time. I liked those shoes! They were new brown brogues. Cost me a pretty penny, too. I bought them from a right fancy shoe shop near Trinity College... don't tell me the name, I reckon I can get it back....' He closed his eyes briefly, screwing them tightly and frowning, then opened them again with a look of triumph. 'Yes! Tranter's. I bought them in Tranter's of Trinity Street.'

That, at least, made him smile a little, to Vita's relief. 'There,' she said, 'that certainly shows how one memory can lead to another.'

He looked tired now. Vita felt she should do as the fierce nurse had said and leave the patient to rest.

'I remember the name of a shoe shop, but not my own name,' the patient said. 'It is a cruel trick for the memory to play.'

'There is hope. You remember something new every time I see you. But I will leave you to rest now,' Vita said.

The patient fell back on his pillows and closed his eyes.

Vita was surprised to meet Dr Goodman in the long first-floor corridor.

'I thought you were off duty and working on your invention today,' she said.

'There was a glue mishap, so I thought it best to stay

away from home for a while. How is our mystery man?' he asked.

'He still has no recollection of his name, but he has an isolated memory of climbing out of a dark hole,' she said.

'They are not always to be trusted, these strange memories people wake up with,' Goodman said. 'I've heard some extraordinary yarns.'

'But in this case, I think I know where it was.'

She explained briefly about her visit to the station and Merrily Farm.

'You must tell that to the police,' he said. 'They're sending a man. He should be here soon. I noticed a puncture wound on the patient's arm this morning. We have not injected him, so it must have been done it earlier. I'm inclined to think he was drugged.'

'Drugged and thrown down a well?' Vita said. 'It seems hardly credible.'

'Someone wanted rid of him. And they went about it thoroughly.'

'Not thoroughly enough, though, since he survived.'

'They underestimated the dosage, that would be my guess. He is a strong young man, fit and powerfully built. Dosages are never easy to guess.'

'But why would anyone want to?'

'Robbery?'

'It seems a lot of trouble to go to for a robbery.'

'Yes,' he said, 'I agree. But the rest is work for the police. And I have a ward round to make.'

SERGEANT DUNWOODY APPEARED SOON AFTERWARDS, his shiny boots tapping with military precision over the hospital's highly polished floor.

'Is this Ward Two, Miss?' he asked Vita, who was sitting in the corridor, looking again at Atkins' *Pure Mathematics*.

'Yes. Are you here to see the patient who lost his memory?'

'I am.'

'May I speak to you afterwards?'

'About the case?'

'Yes.'

'Speak to me now, while I catch my breath,' said the officer. He was a tall man, but also rotund, and puffing a little from the exertion of the stairs. He eased himself into the seat beside her and stroked his large, dark moustache. 'I am Sergeant Dunwoody of the Cambridge Constabulary. I am well known here, at the hospital. It was on my beat when I was a young constable. Many's the time I've been called in here to help with a rowdy patient, or catch an intruder up to no good in the night. That was a few years ago, mind you. I've never come across a case of memory loss before, though. And you are?'

'Vita Carew. I was told that he was found at Waterfen station,' Vita said. 'So I went there this morning and spoke to the crossing keeper.'

'Did you indeed?' said the policeman with a wry smile. 'Thought you'd carry out a few little inquiries on your own, I expect? Because the slow old police officers might miss something.'

Vita blinked at him. 'No, I didn't mean to imply that. I was just curious on the patient's behalf,' she said.

'I'm sure you meant well,' said Dunwoody. He reached into his breast pocket and pulled out a notebook and pencil, licking the tip of the pencil and opening the notebook at a new page. 'We in the police force generally find that well-intentioned amateurs blundering about asking questions are more likely to muddy matters and cause confusion. But let's hear whatever it was you discovered.'

'The crossing keeper showed me a drove road that runs beside the line. I followed it as far as the first farm. It's called Merrily Farm.'

Dunwoody appeared to listen, but wrote nothing. 'Yes,' he said. 'Go on.'

'There were tracks, cart tracks leading to a - well, I think it was an old well. A hole in the ground about three feet across. It was bricked like a well. When I came back, the patient said he had remembered something and told me he had been in a cold dark place and had struggled to climb out. It was difficult. He injured his hands and feet.'

'And what makes you think he was in the well you found? Every farm for miles around has a well. Half of them have a disused one, too, I expect. Does he remember anything else? How he got to the well? How long was he in there?'

'No, he remembers nothing else, but there was a footprint in the mud on the drove road that leads to the station. The print of a large bare foot. He was found without shoes.'

Vita flicked through her own notebook, pulling it from her bag, and showed Dunwoody the sketch she had made of the footprints. He looked at it from several angles.

'That could be anything at all,' he said. 'A dog could have made that. Or a badger.'

'No, look...' she tried to point out the shape, but Dunwoody shook his head. 'I found these, they were along the track I followed too.' Vita found her handkerchief and showed Dunwoody the slips of paper she had picked up. They had partially dried. They both peered at the scraps of paper. Some had the blotted and faded traces of handwriting on them, but no complete words were legible.

'That looks like a prescription,' Dr Goodwin said. He was

looking over Vita's shoulder, having returned without either the policeman or Vita noticing. They both started.

'How can you say that, Sir?' asked Dunwoody, squinting shortsightedly at the tiny pieces.

'Those partial words - they look like abbreviations used for medicines. '*Mag Sulph*', that one says. Magnesium Sulphate - a cream for treating infections. And you can see the dark blue edge to the page. That's common on a notepad for prescriptions.'

Goodwin introduced himself to the police officer, who stood and shook hands.

'Who would have such a notepad?' Dunwoody asked.

'A doctor or a pharmacist, usually,' Goodman said.

'Perhaps the patient is one of those, then,' Dunwoody suggested. 'Or perhaps they just blew there out of a train window. I should like a word with him now, if I may. It should be a quick visit, since he can't tell me anything. We're shorthanded at the station. They can't spare me for long.'

Goodman returned after a few minutes. 'You were not impressed by Sergeant Dunwoody, to judge from your expression,' he remarked. 'I read in the newspaper that a woman police officer recently joined the force in Cambridge.'

'Well, good luck to her. She will need to be a determined character if Sergeant Dunwoody is anything to go by,' Vita said. 'Did you hear the patient say anything about the dropped pieces of paper?'

'The idea seemed familiar to him. Nothing else, though.'

*V*ita looked again at Atkins' *Pure Mathematics* and wondered whether she should pass the time by attempting a few more of the exercises. Opening where she had left off, at page 85, she read Question 7, which said '*Extract the square root of 1095.61, and find to three places of decimals the value of 4/$\sqrt{5}$ - 1.*'

She concentrated on this for a few moments, then decided to go to Tranter's instead.

TRANTER'S SHOE shop was a single window and doorway tucked between larger shops on Trinity Street. Cambridge was busy with Christmas shoppers wrapped against the cold, hurrying to choose treats and gifts from colourful displays on every side. Shop windows twinkled with decorated trees, festoons of red and green silk, bunches of holly and mistletoe. Families of excited children crowded the pavement outside the toy shop opposite pointing to the bright display of dolls, stuffed animals and painted wooden trains.

By contrast, the small rippled panes of glass in Tranter's bow window displayed only a single pair of gentlemen's brogues with wooden stretchers inside them on a raised walnut stand. They were, even to the untrained eye, quietly magnificent. No price was displayed - a certain sign that Mr Tranter's customers need hardly concern themselves with mere money.

No ladies' footwear was on offer, which made entering a little intimidating, but Vita forced herself forward with the thought of the unfortunate young man whose name was lost, and by her alternative occupation, which was Question 7 on page 85.

A bell rang out as she opened the door, and almost before it had stopped, a trim, grey-haired figure in a leather apron trotted up stairs hidden at the back and emerged behind the counter. He assessed her with a merchant's trained eye before he spoke. When he did, it was with one eyebrow slightly raised behind his gold-rimmed spectacles.

'Good morning, Miss. What can I do for you?'

Vita found that his scrutiny had driven all thoughts from her head. It was only at that moment that she realised how muddy and damp her skirt and boots must look. She had prepared a story, but now all she could say was, 'It is rather complicated.'

This, apparently, intrigued Mr Tranter. Perhaps it had been a quiet day in the business. Perhaps selling shoes - even shoes of the highest quality - to bumptious young undergraduates was not always particularly interesting work. Either way, Mr Tranter did not hurry this unprofitable visitor away. Instead, he moved a stool round the counter for her to sit on, found another for himself, and leaned on his elbows, waiting.

Vita could see no harm in sharing the whole story once she had introduced herself. He listened with interest.

'And you came here to see whether we kept records?'

'Yes.'

'We do, naturally. Our customers have their own form, as we call it, and we make their shoes from it for life. Naturally, we record their names and orders. The problem here is that we have no name to go by.'

'He seemed to suggest that the shoes were fairly new,' Vita said hopefully.

'Even so,' said Mr Tranter.

'And they were brown brogues,' she added.

'That is not particularly helpful either, I'm afraid. I have sold approximately forty pairs of brown brogues in the last three months. They are in high demand. Can you tell me any other details?'

'He is thirty or thereabouts.'

'Ah, so not one of our younger gentleman.'

'No, and they found him wearing tweeds. Good tweeds, apparently.'

'Tweeds. A gentleman with country connections in his thirties. That narrows the field to some extent.'

Thoughtfully, Mr Tranter took off his spectacles and polished them on a silken cloth he took from beneath the counter.

'Oh, and he has a northern accent. Yorkshire, possibly.'

'Does he now?' This was more like it. The shopkeeper raised an index finger significantly, left his seat and disappeared down the back stairs, returning with a leather-bound ledger. He placed it on the counter and read, running his finger down the left-hand column.

Reading upside down, Vita could see it was a list of names and addresses, and line after line of notes in some special shoemaker's shorthand, detailing orders and purchases.

They both jumped as the doorbell rang and a pair of young men in black academic gowns burst into the shop.

'Tranter, sir. We are here to buy my friend Foster-Wallace a pair of your finest brogues!' one of them declared.

Three customers in the tiny shop were too many. Vita knew it was time to leave. Tranter, assuming his salesman's manner smoothly, invited the young gentlemen to inspect the shoes in the window for a moment.

'I shall let you know, as soon as I can, Miss,' he said to her aside.

Vita handed him one of her aunt's cards, writing her own name on it first, and squeezed past the young men almost unnoticed. They, a pair of young men on a quest for the finest footwear, took no notice of her at all.

CHAPTER 10

*V*ita hurried back to the hospital, partly because Cambridge's famous east wind was particularly cutting, partly to shake off her irritation. How marvellous it would have been to find the amnesia patient's name so easily, and break the news to him in person. Imagine his gratitude. How impressed Dr Goodman would have been. But no, a spoilt young man had need of *new shoes*!

The sweet, vanilla and cinnamon scented waft of a bakery reminded her that her irritation might also be connected with hunger. She had eaten nothing since breakfast. She decided a currant bun was the cure, and while she was there, she would buy one for the patient and perhaps a spare in case a passing nurse or doctor should feel left out.

So three large and syrupy fruit buns in a paper bag accompanied her as she returned to Addenbrooke's.

Just outside the ward, a man in a greatcoat stood hesitantly in the corridor. He carried his weatherbeaten hat under one arm and looked anxiously about him.

'Excuse me, Miss. Is this the ward where the lost man is? The one from the newspaper?' he asked Vita. He continued without waiting for an answer. 'Only I think I know him. The policeman said I should come here. Hospitals! I never like them. It's the smell. It makes me nervous.'

'I imagine it would be best to speak to his doctors before you go in,' Vita said.

'Yes, I expect you'd be right.'

The man was in his forties. A countryman dressed for outdoors, mud generously spattered about his coat and boots. The smell of the stables on his clothes. He looked about uncomfortably.

At that moment, Goodman came out of the ward with the neurology specialist, Dr McCardle. Vita stepped forward and presented the new visitor. McCardle turned to him with great curiosity.

'You know him?' he said.

'I believe I do, sir. I saw it in the newspaper. I believe he is the young doctor from Halsey. He has not returned to his lodgings or come to his patients for two days. People were wondering…'

'Tell me your name,' McCardle said, holding his hand up to stop the man.

'Jack Bulman, sir. I drive the cart from Halsey to Little-port. On Thursdays I come to market here in Cambridge. I was getting ready to go back this afternoon, when I stopped for my tea. I bought the evening paper to read, and I saw this here.' He produced a folded newspaper from a deep pocket and pointed to an item with a gnarled and grimy finger. The headline was 'Unknown Man found on Station'.

The doctor stepped forward to peer at the story.

'Well,' Jack Bulman said, 'as soon as I seen that, I says to myself, that man sounds like our Dr Linn. So I goes to the policeman by the market there, and he says to come up here to the hospital. That old boy's had a knock on his head and doesn't know his own name until someone tells him it. That's a pitiful thing, I reckon. Pitiful.'

'And do you know Dr Linn personally? Could you identify him if you saw him?' asked McCardle.

'Oh easily. He come to my sister when her cough was bad. Fixed her up with some wonderful cough mixture. Everyone in the village knows Dr Linn. He can't do enough for you. Very good man, he is. Very kind to an old lady we had lodging. Better than his boss by miles is Dr Linn, even though he's only a young 'un. He's very popular.'

The doctor looked back at the carter in surprise.

'You should certainly come and see him to confirm that he is the man you know,' said McCardle, 'but he has been through a series of shocks already, so I need to prepare him for such important news. Please wait here.'

The doctor went back into the ward. Vita was left in the corridor with Jack Bulman.

'I hate to think of anything bad happening to Dr Linn. It says in the paper he was beaten and left for dead. I can't hardly believe it,' he remarked. 'Makes you think nobody's safe anymore. That'd be thieves, I s'pose.'

'Nobody knows what happened,' Vita said. They sat side by side in the corridor.

'It's a terrible thing. I dread to think what they'll say in the village.'

'He is a popular doctor, then, Dr Linn?' Vita asked.

'He is now. Yes, indeed. When he first came, we all wondered. Nobody was too eager to take a chance on a new doctor, in case of him being a bit green, like. And he looks very young, this one, even if he has all the letters after his name. But his boss, Potter, is not...' the carter glanced at Vita, checking to see that she would take this in the right way, '... well, he's not much liked in the village. He has a lot of upper-crust patients - they come from all over, and he goes off taking care of them and their nervous conditions - he knows all about that sort of thing - for days on end, but he i'n't so interested in us and our ordinary old aches and pains. Not much money in that, I s'pose. I hope I'm not speaking out of turn.' He looked down at his cracked and muddy boots, then added, 'and as for Miss Finch, the old vicar's daughter who looks after his house and organises his calls and such like, nobody's got a good word to say for her. She's always been fearsome.'

'But Dr Linn...?' Vita prompted.

'Dr Linn was different right from the start. He comes out day and night in all weathers on that old bone shaker bicycle of his. Remembers you and what you had wrong. Asks after my sister whenever I see him. And now to think of him in the hospital, not even knowing his own name. That's terrible. Nora will break her heart when I tell her.'

McCardle returned and beckoned to the carter, leading him towards the ward.

Vita longed to follow, but had no justification for doing so. She heard McCardle tell Jack Bulman they would just look in on the patient from the door at first, and say nothing until Bulman had confirmed whether the patient truly was the missing doctor.

'I shall do whatever you think best, sir,' Bulman said.

After they had entered the ward, Vita tried to go back to the square root of 1065.91.

$\mathcal{T}$he buns were rich, their syrup was oozing through the paper bag. Vita wondered whether it would be possible to eat one in the hospital corridor without making an embarrassingly obvious mess, but had to accept that it would not. Leaving the spot was out of the question when the patient was so close to finding his identity. The buns would have to wait.

How did a square root work? She ought to know, but who could think of square roots when a man nearby was about to have his life returned to him?

'I'm looking for Ward Two. Is this it?'

A young woman in a blue beret and a heavy woollen nurse's cape had hurried over without Vita noticing. She was muffled against the weather, and what could be seen of her face above her scarf was anxious to the point of being tearful.

'Yes, this is Two,' Vita told her.

'Do you know it?'

'Yes, as a visitor.'

'Do you know anything about the patient they brought in

this morning? The man who was found on the station?' The young woman sat down beside Vita and spoke urgently.

'I have spent some time with him today,' Vita said.

'Do you know him?'

'No, I simply spoke to him. His doctor thought talking to someone might help him remember.'

'And did he? Did he remember anything?'

'Very little, I'm afraid,' Vita said.

'Is he a sandy-haired man? With freckles? Does he have a wave in his hair and blue eyes?' the new arrival asked, looking anxiously at Vita.

'Yes. It sounds as if you know him.'

'I think I do.'

'Somebody else has just gone in to identify him. A carter from a place called Halsey,' Vita told her.

'Yes, Halsey is where he is employed. His name is Linn, Gerald Linn. He is a junior doctor at the medical practice there.'

So relieved was the young woman at this confirmation that she had to pause, pull a handkerchief from a pocket and dab her eyes. When she had caught her breath, she said, 'I have been so worried. I always receive a note from him on a Wednesday, but I heard nothing yesterday. Then just now I read this terrible story in the newspaper. At first I thought, no, it cannot be him, it cannot be Gerald. But he never misses a letter. We usually arrange to meet, you see, on a Thursday, when he comes to town.' She paused for a few moments, unable to do more than dab her eyes.

'You must have been worried,' Vita said, gently.

'He has told me several things recently that gave me cause for concern. I could not shake off the feeling that some-thing was wrong.' The young woman broke off and took a deep breath. 'I apologise. I have no business telling you all this. We haven't been introduced. My name is Jane Douglas. I am a nurse at the cottage hospital in Cherry Hinton.'

'Vita Carew. One of the doctors asked me to sit with and speak to the patient because I have a little experience of injuries to the brain. My brother, Edward, had one. Dr McCardle operated.'

'Operated on his brain?' Jane asked, surprised. 'Here at the hospital?'

'No, it was at home. I live in Eden Street.'

'I am sorry to hear your brother was hurt,' said the newcomer.

'He has recovered well,' Vita told her.

'Can you tell me how Gerald is, please? Miss Carew. I long to know. Will they let me see him?'

'I'm sure they will. They will be out soon, I expect. He is recovering from his physical injuries, but when I saw him earlier, he was still at a loss to remember very much about what had happened. He had a dim memory of being in a well and climbing out.'

'How dreadful!'

'But he still had no memory, even of his name. He seems to know nothing of his past life.'

'Poor Gerald. I suppose he will not know me, then. I dread making matters worse for him.'

'How do you know him?'

'I do not know him particularly well. We met a few months ago at the pharmacy in David Street – Gadd's.'

'Yes, I know the place.'

'I go there on a Thursday to collect medicines for the cottage hospital. They order all their medicines from there. The cottage hospital is a charity. Gadd's is rather a grim little place, but the medicines are a little cheaper there, I imagine.'

'Yes, I believe they are.'

'Anyway, Dr Linn also collects the medicines for his practice in Halsey on a Thursday, and our paths crossed several weeks in a row. We struck up a conversation, and, well, we sometimes walked back to the station together.' Jane Douglas seemed a little shy about making this admission. 'Once or twice, Gerald invited me to take a little walk with him recently. We were beginning to know each other, but only just.'

'He made a good impression on you, though,' Vita said.

'He seems a very polite and good-natured person,' Jane said rather carefully, but she smiled for the first time and looked off into the distance at the thought of their meetings.

'Thank you for taking the time, Mr Bulman.'

Both young women jumped at Dr McCardle's voice. They had been too absorbed to notice the men's approach. Bulman saluted Vita as he passed and strode away.

The women looked at McCardle, waiting.

'His name is Gerald Linn,' the doctor declared, but immediately looked alarmed as the announcement caused the young woman sitting next to Vita to gasp and cover her face with her hands.

'What have we here?' he asked.

'This is Jane Douglas. She is a friend of Dr Linn's,' Vita explained.

CHAPTER 12

'*I* should not like to disturb him - upset him further, I mean,' Jane said. 'You have his identity now, perhaps it is too soon for anyone else to meet him.'

But McCardle, looking serious, urged her on. 'He did not recognise his name. He repeated it a few times and thought it sounded familiar, but it did not seem to prompt any further recovery of his memory. Seeing you - a friend - might prompt him. If you feel able, I would encourage you to visit.'

Jane Douglas stood, but then turned back to Vita.

'Miss Carew, would you come with me? I rushed here, but my courage is failing now,' Jane said, turning to Vita.

'Of course,' Vita said.

'I do not know Gerald well. It seems strange to be thrust into such an important moment of his life - and such a dramatic and terrible one.'

'Yes,' Vita told her, 'I think I understand.'

'Of course, I want to do all I can to help.'

McCardle glanced at his pocket watch. 'I will take you in, Ladies, but I have a ward round in a few minutes. This patient is fascinating, but he is also taking up more of my time than I can spare. I suggest I go in first and prepare him a little, then you follow. It might be a good idea not to introduce yourself, Miss Douglas. It will test whether seeing you is enough to prompt his memory sufficiently to retrieve your name.'

The ladies paused outside the door of the side room while the doctor went ahead. Jane, stiff and clasping her gloved hands together, looked after him.

McCardle re-appeared. 'I have told him only that someone else who knows him has called to visit. He is calm. I shall be interested to hear how he reacts, but do not stay too long. All this is exhausting for him. Leave if he seems tired.'

Vita led the way, Jane almost hiding behind her.

The patient was sitting up, looking blankly towards the window.

'I believe you now have a name,' Vita said, approaching the bed.

'I have. It seems I am Gerald Linn. A medical doctor.'

'Has anything else come back to you?'

'Not really. The name seems familiar, and I suppose I feel no surprise that I am a doctor - that feels true. But if they told me I was a dancer or a mechanic, I might have felt the same.'

Vita had imagined the name would be a happier discovery than this. The patient looked out of the window and watched the snow falling with a troubled expression. The afternoon light was already fading.

Turning back, his attention was drawn to Jane. His face changed and expressed a sudden energetic delight. He sat up from his pillows and reached his hand towards her, but then looked doubtful again. 'Who is this lady?' he asked, smiling at Vita. 'Do I know her?'

Jane stepped forward and stood at his bedside. He continued to look at her with radiant pleasure, smiling.

'Please forgive me,' he said at last. 'I feel I know your face, but I cannot bring a name to mind. Forgive me, please.'

'It is Jane,' she said.

'Jane!' he enjoyed knowing this, and said it several times to himself. 'Jane. Jane. Yes, it seems well-known to me. Will you stay? Please bring a chair, Jane. Sit and talk to me for a while.'

Vita brought another chair over, Jane taking the one closest to the bed. The patient seemed enchanted by this new visitor. He reached out suddenly and took her hand with both of his, as if an urgent thought had occurred.

'Jane! Are we married? Are you my wife, Jane?'

Jane looked nervously at Vita before saying, 'No, we are not married, Gerald.'

He looked disappointed. 'A pity!' he said. 'You are not a sister or a close relative of mine, are you, Jane?' He was still clasping her hand, his bandages covering her glove.

'I am a friend,' Jane said quickly.

This answer pleased Dr Linn. 'A friend! That is promising. Where did we meet?'

'We met at a pharmacy called Gadd's. You dropped a box on my foot, as a matter of fact.'

'How rude of me! I apologise,' said the patient.

'You apologised many times that day. And since. There is no need for further apology. It was an accident, and I was unharmed.'

'Good! Did I buy you lunch to compensate? I hope I did.'

'You offered, but I declined,' she told him.

'Surely I did not take no for an answer, Jane. Please tell me I tried earnestly to persuade you to meet on another occasion.'

Jane was beginning now to smile, despite herself.

'You did persuade me, as it happens,' she told him. 'We went to the Copper Kettle the following week.'

'The Copper Kettle! I have no recollection of the place, but I feel certain it is an excellent choice.' He looked down to where their hands lay together on the bedcover. 'Have I proposed marriage to you yet, Jane?'

Jane resumed her serious face. 'Marriage has not been discussed,' she said. 'We hardly know one another. We have been friends for only a few weeks.'

'Of course,' he said, 'I should have remembered.' He seemed saddened, but looking back at Jane cheered him again. 'Will you stay and talk? If I speak out of turn, I apologise.'

'I will stay, of course,' Jane said, 'but not for long this time. Dr McCardle says you are not to be tired. I am a nurse, Gerald. I always obey a doctor's orders.'

He leaned back on his pillows, looking tired. 'I am a doctor too,' he said.

'Not at present. At present, Dr Linn, you are the patient.'

Vita left them in quiet conversation, but she could tell that Jane would soon leave her friend to rest.

As Vita returned to the row of chairs in the corridor, she saw a porter pushing a wheeled stretcher pause as her bag of buns caught his eye. He bent and picked it up, opening the bag to peer inside.

'Ooh!' he said, to nobody in particular, 'they look like tasty buns!'

He was a thin man. The brown overall he wore, being of a standard size, hung loose about him. The sleeves had to be rolled at the cuffs.

'Yes, they do.' Vita said.

The man jumped and looked guilty. 'I was only looking. I thought someone had left them here. Forgotten them and gone home or something. They were brought today. They seem fresh. Did you see someone leave this bag here, Miss?'

'Could you eat them yourself?' Vita asked him.

'I'd take them home. A little Christmas treat for my lads. They'd love that. But what if the owner comes back?'

'I'm sure the owner would like you to have them,' she said. 'If anyone complains, I'll take responsibility.'

The porter grinned. He placed the bag of buns on his stretcher as if it was an injured patient and wheeled them away, whistling.

CHAPTER 13

*J*t had long been dark by the time Vita reached home that evening. She was hungry and cold, her coat and boots wet from the sleet and snow that had fallen all day.

From the slushy pavement in front of 144 Eden Street, there was a view down into the basement kitchen. Through the railings, Vita glimpsed a lively discussion under way between the chef, Monsieur Picard, and her aunt.

Monsieur Picard - usually known simply as *Monsieur* - had come to Eden Street from a grand country house. He cooked for Mrs Brocklehurst once or twice a week as a favour, expecting free rein in the kitchen. The results were superb, making Aunt Louisa's dinners famous in Cambridge circles. Nonetheless, there were occasional differences of opinion between the hostess and her chef.

Even from the street outside, it was plain to Vita that they were, that particular evening, at loggerheads.

She crept indoors, hoping to avoid being drawn in, only to encounter her aunt rushing up the back stairs in ill-disguised fury.

'Oh, that man!' she cried. 'I am a perfectly reasonable woman, Vita, am I not?'

'Of course you are, Aunt,' Vita said, hanging up her coat and backing away, hoping to slip up to her room.

'Christmas pudding! That is all I ask. It is not too much to ask for Christmas pudding to be served at a Christmas Eve dinner, surely?'

'Of course not. Does Monsieur disagree?'

'He says he will not serve it. It is not edible, he says.'

'Not edible?'

'Not according to him. Nobody could possibly want to eat it, he says. It is a foul black bolus, he says. He would not feed it to cattle.'

Vita composed her face, which was tempted to smile.

'Don't you dare laugh!' cried her aunt. 'He is a tyrant! This is our family recipe. Tabitha and I prepared it weeks ago. It is matured to perfection. This pudding is a tradition, and I intended to uphold it.'

'Good for you!' Vita said.

'I want it served with brandy sauce and I want it lit and decorated with holly and carried, in flames, to the table in the dark!'

'Quite right!' Vita told her, having now to press her hand over her mouth for fear of bursting out laughing.

'This is no laughing matter, Vita. I must assert myself or this man will force an entirely French Christmas dinner upon my guests. French food is all very well. I have conceded to his lobster, I have submitted to his oysters, we shall even eat roast beef rather than goose because that is what Monsieur advises. But I go no further! We shall have Christmas pudding. We shall!'

From down in the kitchen, a great crashing of pans signalled the chef's feelings on the matter. Aunt Louisa's eyes narrowed, but she stood tall and took a deep breath. 'Tabitha has prepared a shepherd's pie tonight because Monsieur says he is too busy. He has, however, left some of his special onion soup. It will be on the table in ten minutes.'

Further reverberations echoed from below as the two ladies made their way to the dining room. They both did their best to ignore the noise. Besides, it had been a busy day, and Vita had a lot to tell her aunt.

CHAPTER 14

*M*iss Finch looked up to see her employer in his greatcoat, bag in hand. 'A house call? There is none in the diary.'

'I said I would call on Mrs Palmer,' he said without stopping.

'You have visited her daily for the past week. I must send the invoice to Lady Celia today. You know her terms. She will pay promptly when matters are completed.'

'I am not ready to *complete matters*,' he said, standing with his back to her and a hand on the front door.

'You don't normally delay.'

He turned and spoke angrily, but quietly. They could both hear the other doctor's patients behind a waiting room door to their right. 'You speak as if it were the most natural thing on earth.'

'Death *is* the most natural thing on earth,' she replied, equally quietly.

'Natural death is, yes.'

'Death in advanced old age, after a long retirement. It is not only natural, but a positive blessing.'

'She is a pleasant and interesting old lady,' he said. 'She gives me boiled sweets.'

'Boiled sweets? Lucian! This is no time to grow sentimental. We need the fee from Lady Celia.'

'There is more than enough in the bank, surely, without this trifling amount?' He avoided her eye.

'I have calculated very precisely. New lives in new countries. It all *costs money*.'

'And is it only about money to you?'

'Oh, not that! Not now!'

He shrugged. 'I like the old lady. We play Ludo. Her father taught her. He was in the Merchant Navy.'

Miss Finch stood, slamming the book on her desk closed. She spoke in a furious whisper. 'If we are to leave without a backward look, we must have the fee for this last case to cover the added expense of *removing Dr Linn*. I must pay the wretched farmer you recruited in advance. You know that! If you will just finish what Lady Celia asks today, all will be in order.'

Potter stood at the door a moment longer, then turned irritably back to his consulting room, where he unlocked a medicine cabinet and added several items from it to his bag.

CHAPTER 15

FRIDAY, DECEMBER 23RD

*T*abitha was just serving breakfast when the doorbell rang several times, urgently.

Since the maid had her hands full, Vita opened the front door. She found Jane Douglas in her blue beret and cape standing on the doorstep in a state of acute anxiety.

'May I speak to you, Miss Carew? It is most urgent.'

'Of course,' Vita led her into the parlour.

'I have interrupted. I do apologise,' Jane said. She was clutching a letter. 'This was delivered to the nurse's home this morning. It is from Gerald. He must have posted it before he went missing. Vita, it is a frightening letter. I had to show it to someone. I hope you don't mind me bringing it here. I know so few people in Cambridge. I remembered you lived in Eden Street and your neighbour directed me. Would you read it, please? I am at a loss to know what to do.'

Vita took the letter from its envelope. It was several pages long. She unfolded it and read:

63

The Black Horse, Halsey
Tuesday, December 20th 1904

DEAR JANE,

I propose we visit the Botanical Gardens on Thursday.
The trees and lawns will be grand, even in winter, and there is
a warm tea room in case of snow. Time in your company is a
cheerful thought.

(I wrote the above yesterday. Matters have changed since
then.)

Jane, I have just hidden a blue accounts ledger by
securing it to the underside of the lower drawer of the oak
wardrobe in my room. It will only be found if the drawer is
pulled right out and turned over. I will try to explain, but time
is pressing. I must hurry to catch the last post.

Patients in Halsey now speak to me openly about Potter.
They complain of his rudeness; his turning them away or
refusing to call, even in emergency cases. Far worse, they
call him a 'hastener'. One old man told me about his dying
wife, saying, 'Potter hastened her away before her time. He's
known for it in these parts, Sir.'

Known for it! I would have put this down to an elderly
man's misunderstanding of medicine, but he wasn't alone.
Several other 'hastenings' are openly spoken of in the village.

Last week, Miss Bulmer, the sister of the carter down the
lane, wanted me to see Mrs Palmer, an old lady who boards
with her. She could not rouse her.

I found Mrs Palmer lying unconscious after taking a new
medicine Potter had prescribed. It was a strong tincture of
laudanum from Gadd's. Potter had prescribed a dose of
twenty drops. As you know, Jane, a frail elderly patient would
almost certainly be killed by such a dose.

I sat with Mrs Palmer until the small hours, but there was nothing I could do. She died.

When I told Potter the next day, he was outraged. He threatened me with the wrath of the local medical committee and the General Medical Council. Mrs Palmer was one of his private patients. I had interfered.

Potter drinks. He is not the first doctor to drink too much, or the first to hide it with the help of a loyal retainer. Miss Finch is Potter's right hand; his confidante. She alone has access to all accounts, appointment books and medical notes.

When Potter called her upstairs this morning, she left papers in open view on her desk. I had never seen this before. Among them was the ledger I have just hidden.

It lists patients' names over a period of more than twenty years, together with the date of their death, and the fees charged. The last name inscribed is that of Emily Palmer, aged seventy-seven. Her name is paired with that of Lady Celia Lampton.

I have read and re-read this ledger, unable for a long time to force myself to the conclusion I still resist: that this is what Halsey villagers mean by Potter being a 'hastener'. He dispatches ordinary patients he grows tired of treating, but in addition to that, he takes fees, large fees, to rid wealthy families of people they find inconvenient.

The ledger is the proof. Miss Finch writes everything down.

Jane, I am a proud Yorkshireman. Melodrama does not suit me. Miss Finch - neat, well-organised Miss Finch - will know this ledger is missing. I am the only possible suspect. She and Potter know where to find me. I live across the street. If Potter has done away with more than three dozen people so far, it is fair to assume that he would not hesitate to add one more. This letter and the ledger are evidence that could convict him of murder.

I therefore end in haste and hurry this to the letterbox before I can be prevented. The ledger is too large to post, so I have hidden it.

I hope that I shall appear as usual at Gadd's in plenty of time to have the pleasure of a stroll with you in the Botanical Gardens. If I do, we shall be able to laugh together at these colourful imaginings of mine. If I do not appear, please take this letter to the police and tell them where to find the ledger.

Forgive the length of this letter, and my hasty scrawl. I hurry to record what I can while I still have the chance. If any of this frightens you, Jane, I apologise. We are not well acquainted yet, but what little I know of you tells me that besides being beautiful enough to take my breath away, you are trustworthy, calm, level-headed and brave - as all very best nurses are. I know I am right to trust you.

Yours in haste,
Gerald Linn MD

CHAPTER 16

*J*ane was introduced and Aunt Louisa's breakfast toast grew cold as she read the letter.

'Goodness!' she exclaimed. 'What do you make of this, Miss Douglas?'

'I am inclined to take Gerald - Dr Linn - at his word,' Jane said, 'he had mentioned the difficult atmosphere at Dr Potter's practice before, but he had never said anything about such dreadful suspicions.'

'What will you do?'

'I shall fetch the ledger he mentions from Halsey,' Jane said, 'as he asks.'

'And I suppose you, Vita, will offer to accompany Jane?'

Vita had been expecting opposition to this, and was surprised to hear her aunt voice the idea herself.

'I shall, if Jane will allow it,' she said. 'A witness might be useful.'

Jane nodded agreement.

Aunt Louisa looked the two younger women up and down. 'Should this letter not be taken straight to the police?'

'Sergeant Dunwoody was not keen to listen to me before.

67

I wonder how seriously they will take this. Or how rapidly their men can be deployed so close to the Christmas holiday,' Vita said.

'How will you get to this place - Halsey, is it called? Where is it?'

'It is a few miles outside Littleport. A straightforward journey on the train,' Jane told her.

'I shall insist that you take the whistle with you,' Aunt Louisa said. 'How am I to know if you're safe? If this doctor and his assistant are acting as this letter suggests, it could be very dangerous to cross them.'

The last time Vita had tried to use this whistle in an emergency, it had failed to make any sound whatsoever, but she did not like to remind her aunt of this detail.

'I could leave this letter with you, Mrs Brocklehurst, if you would be willing to keep it,' Jane said. 'If we do not return by early evening - say six o'clock - you could take it to the police yourself, and alert them to our non-return at the same time.'

Aunt Louisa still looked uncertain. 'What would your parents say of such a venture, Miss Douglas?' she asked.

Jane smiled. 'My parents are on a geographical survey expedition in the mountains of Mongolia,' she said. 'I have been brought up to be as independent as possible. They would certainly trust my judgement.'

At this, Aunt Louisa could only blink and fetch the silver whistle from her cabinet drawer.

CHAPTER 17

*G*add's Pharmacy was a drab shopfront in one of Cambridge's narrower side streets with dusty glass bottles in the window. Jane still needed to collect the usual order for the cottage hospital, so she and Vita called there on the way to the station.

As they approached, Vita said, 'Jane, if Dr Potter orders all his medicines from Gadd's, those he uses in the shadier side of his private practice might be part of his regular order. It would be interesting to know what they are.'

'Orders are put on a side shelf ready for collection. Potter's package is usually waiting on the shelf next to the one for the cottage hospital. That is how Dr Linn and I came to meet. Perhaps I could take Potter's box, if it's there.'

'Gadd will notice if you take two packages, surely?'

'He might, but he is not usually very attentive.'

'If you distracted him, I might be able to slip Potter's box out of the shop myself,' Vita suggested. 'What does the package Dr Linn usually collects look like?' Vita asked, struck by a sudden idea.

'Just a brown carton. There is nothing particular about it,' Jane told her. 'I suppose it is about the size of a shoe box.'

'So if we could find a similar carton, we could substitute it?' suggested Vita.

'Yes, but where - ?' Jane began, but when she looked, Vita had gone. She had ducked into the nearest shop.

Puzzled, Jane looked into the window at the single pair of shoes on display.

A moment later, Vita came out with a plain brown shoe box. 'Will this do?' she asked.

It would have to. They hurried on. It was cold enough for their breath to cloud around them.

Gadd himself had the flat nose and jug-eared look of an unlucky prize fighter. He was notoriously ungracious to his customers and always seemed to emerge from his back room as if something far more interesting was going on there. But even Gadd's usual hostility was softened by the beauty of Jane Douglas. He glanced briefly at Vita, but then switched all his attention towards Jane with an unpractised attempt at a smile.

'Everything is on the shelf, ready, Miss,' he said, pointing to a shelf on one side where a row of packages stood ready for collection. 'Everything on the list. It's all there, ready and waiting for you, as usual.'

'Thank you, Mr Gadd,' Jane said. With a tiny eye signal to Vita, she walked up to Gadd's counter instead of going to collect the package. 'I wonder if you have any Gentian Violet? I was asked to collect a bottle, while I'm here.'

'Oh yes, Miss, certainly,' Gadd said with oily ingratiation, and turned to the shelves behind.

Jane nodded her head towards the shelf where the medicines were awaiting collection. Vita feigned interest in a collection of surgical instruments in a display at the back of the shop, then stepped over and doing her best to stand so that Gadd's view was blocked, slid the box labelled 'Potter' off the shelf and replaced it with the empty shoebox. Potter's box was heavier than she had expected, and to her horror it rattled and clinked as she lifted it, glass bottles shifting inside. She daren't look to see if Gadd had heard or reacted, but she heard Jane laugh as if to cover the sound.

'You know, I think I might even take a second bottle, Mr Gadd, if it's not too much trouble,' Vita heard Jane say.

'Oh no, it's no trouble *at all*, Miss,' Gadd replied.

MOMENTS LATER, the two women were hurrying towards the station. The shout they feared from the pharmacist never came.

CHAPTER 18

*I*t was tempting to open Potter's box of medicines at the station, but that could not be done without arousing unwanted interest and besides, they were in a hurry. Vita left it with the Left Luggage clerk and the women hurried onto the departing King's Lynn train with moments to spare.

As they drew close to Waterfen, Jane looked out of the window and said, 'Isn't this the place where they found Gerald?'

'Yes, it is,' Vita told her. 'The crossing keeper told me he was on the down platform across there.'

'How did he come to be there? It is the middle of nowhere.'

'The keeper was puzzled himself. He had not heard a cart between the time he checked the platform after the last train and the time Gerald was found. All he noticed was that the gate over there - look you can just see it - an overgrown gate, might have been disturbed.'

'Opened?'

'He didn't even know. It just looked different, he said.'

The two women peered out of the window. The over-grown drove road was barely visible, but knowing it was there, they could just make it out, running alongside the railway line.

'I suppose the road is used by farmers,' Jane said. 'It is bleak in this weather.'

'And lonely in all weathers.' Vita pointed. 'That's where I found the old well.'

'And you think that's is where Gerald was?'

'I do. I told Sergeant Dunwoody, but he showed no interest. He didn't write down anything I said.'

'Do the police officers have their own theories?' Jane asked. 'Is that why they are not interested in what you had to say?'

'I think it was more that the Sergeant decided my amateur ideas were not to be taken seriously,' Vita said, with a sigh.

'All the more reason to fetch this ledger ourselves,' Jane said. 'If we just handed Gerald's letter over to Sergeant Dunwoody, he might think that was just another girlish flight of fancy.'

'They could not dismiss the letter, but even if the police did take action, it would probably not be fast. They are short of men at Christmas time. He mentioned that several times.'

They both looked out of the windows at the flat fenland landscape under the heavy grey sky.

'If Potter has done this,' Jane said. 'If he really has done away with many patients over the years, and accumulated a fortune in doing so, wouldn't he be well on the way to France or Ireland or somewhere else overseas by now?'

'He might be, if he and Miss Finch were calmly putting a joint plan into action. His drinking suggests matters are not so orderly, though.' Vita shuddered. The train was cold, the land-scape outside wintery, as if reflecting their grim thoughts.

'You think they are conspirators?' Jane asked.

'How could it be otherwise? Miss Finch has kept a secret ledger recording every - what was the word Dr Linn used? - every '*hastening*' Potter has carried out. She's worked closely with him for years. She must have had full knowledge. Whether any of the fees passed to her, we can only guess.'

'I don't know whether I believe any of this yet,' Jane said.

'Why would a doctor resort to this?' Vita said.

'To murdering their patients?'

'Yes. Why would a doctor end up killing people instead of saving their lives?'

Jane looked at Vita. 'I have not been nursing long,' she said, 'but I have already witnessed cases where a patient's life is a burden to them. They are suffering unendurable pain, for example, and have no hope of recovery. I have not seen a doctor 'hasten' a patient into the next life, but I have seen occasions where I would not have blamed one if he had.'

'You think these were mercy killings, then?'

'I don't know. It's one possibility,' Jane said.

Both women fell silent for a few minutes. They watched the countryside passing outside.

'I am from the West Country,' Vita finally said. 'I must admit that I find the fen landscape flat and foreboding in winter.'

Jane laughed, 'I agree,' she said, 'I always feel a few rolling hills would cheer the place up a great deal. But no doubt the broad skies have their appeal, when they are not as grey as they are today.'

The carriage they took from Littleport station was at least covered. It took them out of the town and along a straight hedged road. The landscape was slowly enveloped in grey snow-bearing cloud, closing around them until even the sounds of the horse's hooves were muffled. A stiff wind tossed flurries of snow across the road ahead.

Once they reached Halsey, the sign of the Black Horse was soon in view. Paying the driver, the two women hurried into the inn, glad of its light and warmth. It was not, otherwise, a very appealing place, the interior smoky and apparently deserted. But as they looked about for someone to help them, they heard sounds of panic from the room behind. 'I can't move it, Matty!' a woman said in a voice sharp with fear.

Without hesitation, Vita and Jane stepped behind the counter, following the sound. It came from the cellar. Hurrying down the steep steps - more of a ladder - they found a woman sitting on the brick floor and a man bent over her. The woman was holding her leg, which was swollen and bruised.

The pair looked up in surprise.

'I am a nurse,' Jane said. 'perhaps I can help you?'

As she spoke, the woman on the floor swayed and slumped forward.

'What's happening to her?' The man asked, anxiously.

'She is losing consciousness. It's probably the pain,' Vita said.

The two young women went into action together. They laid the woman flat and Jane listened to her breathing.

'I think she has just fainted,' Jane told Vita. She turned to the man. 'Have you some clean cloths or something we could use for a bandage?'

He looked helplessly at her, unable to respond. He seemed transfixed by the unnatural angle of his wife's leg as she lay on the cold flagstones of the cellar.

'We need something clean to tie her leg with,' Vita explained. The man, clearly shocked, only slowly understood.

'There are clean towels,' he said, backing away, unable to take his eyes from his unconscious wife. 'They are upstairs.'

'Yes, fetch some, please,' Vita told him.

He hesitated a moment, then turned away and blundered up the stairs.

'We can bind the legs together to stabilise the break for now,' Jane said, 'but she needs a doctor. She must have fallen on the stairs. It looks like a nasty break.'

She bent over the woman and examined her head and neck. 'I don't think anything else is broken.'

The man returned, his boots clattering down the wooden stairs. He handed Vita a pile of white towels, which she folded one at a time, and handed to Jane. Jane bound them round the patient's legs.

The tension in the dim cellar lessened. The man seemed calmer. 'This is my doing,' he told them. I should have mended that handrail, it split a week ago. She reminded me about it only yesterday. I'm sorry, Mary, I'm so sorry, my dear,' he told his wife, crouching beside her again.

Vita looked across and could see what he meant. The handrail on one side of the cellar steps had split diagonally, leaving two sharply splintered points. The woman must have lost her footing and reached for the rail, only for it to fall open.

A quiet groan showed the woman was regaining consciousness. She opened her eyes and looked in confusion at the two women kneeling over her. Turning her head, she seemed to search for her husband.

'What happened, Matty?' she asked.

'I'm here, my dear,' he told her. 'You fell and you hurt your leg. These young ladies are putting you to rights.'

'Oh yes,' she said. 'I fell.'

TWENTY MINUTES LATER, having shifted the landlady up the cellar steps one painful rung at a time, all four of them were in the kitchen. Introductions had been made. The kettle was on for a cup of tea and Mary's damaged leg was resting, still bound to the other, on a cushion.

'You should call a doctor, Mr Barnes. We've stopped the break from moving, as best we can, but a physician needs to set it properly. There is a medical practice in the village, I believe,' Jane said.

'I shall send Toby from next door to ride for Dr Callendar in Littleport,' the landlord said. He walked to the back door, threw it open and yelled the boy's name, telling him to come quick.

'You ladies are very skilled,' Mrs Barnes said. 'You said you were a nurse, Miss Douglas?'

'Yes, at the cottage hospital in Cherry Hinton.'

'And you, Miss Carew?'

'I have only first aid training.'

'Well, between the two of you, I could hardly have been luckier, could I, Dan? I don't know what we should have done without you.'

'But there is a doctor here in the village?' Vita said, taking up her friend's line of questioning.

The landlord made a face. 'There are two. That's to say, there used to be two. One of them has gone off somewhere. The other one, well, I'd have run for him, but I saw him leave in his carriage earlier. His house is opposite. Not that Potter's much good in a crisis.'

'He hates being called out,' Mrs Barnes explained. 'He's been known to refuse to come. He doesn't like to be inconvenienced. And he charges a fortune.'

'He is not popular, this doctor, then?'

'Nobody likes him,' Matthew Barnes said. 'He's been here for years, but he sees mostly fancy patients in big houses nowadays. The young one was alright, but he's gone off and nobody knows where.'

'We know because he boards here with us, you see,' Mary Barnes told them. 'Nice young man, Dr Linn, he sees the people in the village.'

'Jane knows Dr Linn,' Vita said.

The landlord and his wife looked at Jane expectantly.

'He's in the hospital. He had an accident. He is getting better, but his memory has been damaged. We came to see if there was anything in his room that might help him recover it,' Jane said, 'if you would allow us to look in his room, that is.'

'The poor man! Well, of course you can look in his room,' said Mrs Barnes. 'We thought he'd gone off on a trip or a holiday, perhaps. Potter makes his life difficult. People have overheard him shouting at him in the surgery. Potter's juniors rarely last long. We've had two staying here, neither of them lasted longer than their three months' probation.'

'But we could look in his room?'

'I can't see the harm in it,' the landlord said, 'though you won't be the first. The woman from the Doctor's, Miss Finch, came over yesterday. Said he'd carried off some papers she needed.'

'We didn't want to let her in,' Mrs Barnes said. 'She's an old dragon and as nosey as could be. I didn't think it was right coming over here poking among a gentleman's belongings, whatever excuse she had. But she's a hard one to say 'no' to.'

'She left in a bad temper. I said, *everything satisfactory, Miss Finch?* and she stormed straight past me. They say in the parlour bar that Miss Finch is only polite to people with a title,' Mr Barnes said, 'but I'm not sure she could be decent to anybody at all these days, title or no. Sharp as a pickaxe, that one.'

'It sounds as if whatever she was looking for, Miss Finch did not find it when she came,' Vita said, once Mr Barnes had let them into Dr Linn's little room and left them to look around.

'Gerald said the ledger was under the drawer in the wardrobe.' Jane stooped and opened the drawer and together they emptied it of several folded blankets. When it was empty, they tried to pulled the drawer out. It took both of their efforts to shift it, but together they slid it clear of the wardrobe and turned it over. There on the underside, wedged between two planks, was a long narrow blue book.

Vita's eye was caught by a movement in a window of the house across the road from the pub. It was set well back from the road, but a large bow window looked down the drive in their direction. Vita could dimly see the figure of a woman in a white blouse and dark skirt standing in the window. She seemed to be looking up at Dr Linn's window. 'Jane, I think that must be Miss Finch. She might want to stop us.'

'I wonder where Potter is?' Jane said.

'I don't know, but we know Miss Finch is eager to have this ledger, so I think we should take it and leave as quickly as we can. I'll ask Mr Barnes to send for the carter.'

They wrapped the book in a shawl and put them into Vita's shoulder bag, before hurrying down to the kitchen.

'Is the doctor on his way?' Jane asked.

'They sent a message up the line from the station. He'll be here directly.'

The landlady was dozing in the warm kitchen. She seemed comfortable enough.

'Mr Barnes,' Vita said, 'I think we have found something that will help Dr Linn a great deal. It might also be what Miss Finch was looking for yesterday. She may not want us to take this. She may try to intercept us. Can you help us to…'

'… To slip away quickly?' he said. 'Yes. Come out the back way and I'll show you the field path to Bulman's. Miss Finch won't see you from over the road. You should ask Nora Bulman about what happened to her old lodger, too.'

They said goodbye and good luck to their patient and followed the landlord out of his back door. He pointed to a path that led over the field behind the pub to a cottage whose roof and smoking chimney they could just see. 'It's muddy, Ladies, I'm afraid,' he said, 'but if Miss Finch comes here asking, we won't tell her where you went. It is a small favour, after what you have done for my wife.'

CHAPTER 20

*J*ack Bulman came out of his horse's stable as they approached. When they explained what they needed, he sent them into the parlour to wait while he got the cart hitched up. 'My sister Nora'll set you by the fire to keep warm,' he said.

Nora Bulman, a tall woman in her forties with grey hair in a severe bun, was kneading what looked like fruit bread on the kitchen table, but she wiped her floury hands on her apron and offered to make tea. Jane and Vita refused this, but were glad of the warmth of the fire.

'Mr Barnes said we should ask you about the old lady you had staying here,' Vita said, remembering.

'He's an evil man. I know it for certain. I tried to tell people, but nobody would listen.'

'Who is?' Vita asked, taken aback by this sudden declaration. 'What happened? Can you tell us?'

'Potter.' Miss Bulman dusted her hands with flour and began kneading again, pushing the dough away from her and folding it over with more vigour than she had before.

'I'll tell anybody who will listen, Miss. She shouldn't

have died. There was nothing wrong with her. She was a nice old girl. I was fond of her. I used to talk to her in the afternoons, you know, take her up her tea and have a chat with her - keep her company. She had no family, which is why she was here.'

Vita and Jane looked at one another in confusion.

'Was this lady a relative of yours, Miss Bulman?'

At the table, Miss Bulman slapped the kneaded dough into a baking tin and began kneading the next loaf. 'Not a relative, a boarder. We have a room here that we let out. She was a housekeeper in a big house, retired for some years, living in her old room, but they needed it for someone else, so they wanted her out. Potter recommended us. Told them we were good people to board with. We were supposed to be grateful for that, I suppose. He likes to think everyone's beholden to him. They probably paid him for his advice, too. I wouldn't put it past him to take money from the situation. The family from the great house paid us and they probably paid Potter for her medicines and his care of her too.'

Miss Bulman paused and, to their surprise, the young women saw her brush a tear from her cheek with the back of a floury hand. 'She was a nice old thing, Miss Palmer. Friendly. I lost my mother. I never knew a grandmother. It was nice to have her company. When she first come, I thought she might be fussy, like, what with her having been a housekeeper in a grand house. I thought she might be finding fault and feeling she had come down in the world, but she weren't like that. She was just grateful to have somewhere to stay. She liked it here. I made her welcome. She loved my cooking. She liked to sit in the garden on a bright day. She was no trouble. No trouble to anybody.'

They could hear horses' hooves outside as the cart was being readied. Vita again caught Jane's eye, and they exchanged a look of uncertainty, unsure about where this story could be leading.

'What happened to Mrs Palmer?' Vita asked.

Miss Bulman stopped moving, her hands in a soft ball of dough. She looked down at the table. 'She died. Potter killed her.'

In the silence that followed, a gust of wind caused the kitchen fire to flare and crackle.

'Can you be sure of that?'

'All I know is that she was well, her appetite was good, she was up and about, going for walks, doing a bit of sewing, taking an interest. He called on her a few times. He was friendly. He played a game or two of Ludo with her. But then after he'd seen her a few times, she was asleep all the time, drowsy. Not herself any longer at all. He give her medicines - she didn't need them, she wasn't ill, but Doctor knows best, so she swallowed anything he told her to.'

'This is very serious, Miss Bulman,' Vita said.

'It is. I know it is. She is not the only one either. Folk in a place like this are too scared to say anything against a doctor. I told my brother, and he said, don't go spreading that around, you'll need the doctor yourself one day. I even went and told the medical man in Littleport, Dr Callendar. I went there, and I told him to his face what Potter did, but he wouldn't listen. He just said Potter was *a very experienced man*. He didn't want to know. They stick together.'

The kneading was finished. Miss Bulman bent to open the oven door and slid half a dozen loaf tins onto the shelf. She closed it with a clank and straightened up to look at the young women.

'Mrs Palmer had nobody in the world to speak for her. A lifetime of hard work and they sent her away with one little suitcase and that clock.' She pointed to a small carriage clock on the black beam that served as a mantel shelf over the cooking range. 'I know I'm supposed to keep quiet and not ask questions. I'm a spinster lady who makes a living selling a few cakes and taking in lodgers. I've got no schooling. Nobody will listen to me. But I won't be hushed. I asked a few people about Potter. They talk to me. I believe he's been doing this sort of thing for years and years. And Miss Finch, the woman who works for him, she knows all about it.'

'Did you tell the police?' Jane asked.

'I tried to, Miss. I told the sergeant in the police station at Littleport. He said they'd look into it, but I don't think they took any notice.'

Jack's head poked round the door. 'The cart's ready,' he said. 'The cover's up, but you'll need a blanket, the snow's getting worse.'

Nora Bulman scattered flour on her table, ready to knead of the next batch of Christmas loaves. 'Please,' she said, 'if you two young ladies can do anything to stop Potter, I beg you to do it. The police might listen to you. Somebody's got to stop him. I will speak against him in any court. I believe he killed her, killed her carelessly, the way you'd finish off an old hen. It's wrong and he should pay for it. And I'm not afraid of that horrible man or the wicked woman he works with.'

CHAPTER 21

*A*t half past four in the afternoon they found Littleport station quiet and snow-swept, but the waiting room had a fire, so Vita and Jane huddled inside. Someone had put a Christmas tree in a corner and hung a holly wreath over the door. From time to time, Jane, with her cloak wrapped around her, put a head out of the door to see whether anyone had followed from Halsey.

'What could she do, anyway? Miss Finch is not a young woman. She is hardly likely to attack us in public,' Vita said, drying her boots at the fire.

'If she is implicated in Dr Potter's crimes, she has a very great deal to lose, Vita. She could be charged with conspiracy to murder,' Jane reminded her.

Both looked towards Vita's bag, where the ledger was still wrapped in a shawl.

The sound of a train approaching distracted them and they looked out to see the clouds of steam and lights of the Cambridge train approaching. Many carriages were empty, so they climbed into one, and Vita looked out of the window along the platform. One or two other passengers emerged from shelter and climbed aboard. Only one was a woman, but in the steam and the dying light of the winter's afternoon, it was difficult to see her. The train had no corridor, so in a compartment of their own, Vita and Jane felt safe. They unwrapped the ledger as soon as the train pulled away.

Vita was the first to pull the long narrow book from its shawl wrapping, but hesitated, looking at Jane, before opening it. Jane removed her gloves, but made no move towards the ledger. The station master's loud whistle made both of them jump as the train hissed and jolted into motion.

'Doctor Linn must have thought this was very important. You should be the one to open it,' Vita said.

'I dread the contents,' Jane said, 'but we must be practical, I suppose.'

Both continued to look at the ledger where it rested on the seat between them. Neither moved.

'He must have trusted you very much. He told only you its whereabouts.'

Jane ran her hand over her empty gloves, pressing them against her knee. 'We really don't know each other well. A few walks, a shared luncheon. I can't imagine why he felt I was the one to be entrusted with this. Perhaps he doesn't know many other people. Neither of us has lived here for long.'

Neither spoke as the train gained speed and crossed the flat landscape in the dark.

'What I know of Gerald Linn is so little, Vita. The unfortunate young man in the hospital is Gerald, but he is also not Gerald. There is no way of knowing whether he will ever recover his memory. Even if he does, his personality, his character, his very identity might be changed by such an incident. I have worked in a ward where stroke patients and people with head injuries struggled to make long recoveries. It is painfully slow and uncertain.'

'You feel you are drawn into something that is out of all proportion to your brief acquaintance?' Vita suggested.

'Yes, precisely. I'm so glad you can see it,' Jane looked over at Vita. 'Do you think me cold-hearted?'

'No, Jane, not in the least. The circumstances are strange enough to give anyone pause.'

'It would be so easy to play the loving fiancée. I am not his fiancée, Vita. I was a new friend, and we were beginning to know one another. I do not want to act a part just because it might offer him comfort. It would not be kind to him in the end - if I led him to believe something I do not genuinely feel.'

'No, of course,' Vita said. 'When you were speaking to my aunt, you said your parents were geographers, I think. Am I right about that?'

Jane seemed relieved that the subject had been changed. 'Yes, they are in Mongolia on an expedition. I have grown up on their journeys. They always carried me along with them. I have been all over the world.'

'What an unusual and interesting childhood you had,' Vita said.

'I took it for granted, obviously. When I finally came back to England to school, I was astonished that half the girls in my class had never travelled outside the country. Some had never been further than Brighton, twenty miles away. I thought it might be rather pleasant to grow up in one place with a single group of friends. I had always been among adults. Other children found me very odd.'

'And were your parents encouraging when you chose nursing?'

'Encouraging in a distant way. They were in Bolivia at the

time, I think. They trained me in self-sufficiency above all else.'

'Why did you choose it?'

Jane smiled. 'I might ask why you chose to study science, Vita. Another unusual choice. Are you aiming for medicine, eventually?'

'I am, but to be honest, my first year of undergraduate study is so difficult that I am afraid it may be my last.'

'Oh come now,' Jane said. 'Just one more little hill ahead.'

Vita looked at her, confused.

'My mother is famous for urging expeditions over vast mountain ranges by telling them that there is *just one more little hill ahead*,' Jane said. 'It's a form of self-delusion we all need from time to time.'

'Mathematics may genuinely be a mountain range too high for me,' Vita said. 'Shall we have a look at the contents of this ledger?'

'Yes,' Jane said, 'let's!'

Jane took a deep breath and opened the ledger between them on the seat. Vita pulled her glasses from her bag and put them on. Both leaned in.

What they saw was a set of handwritten accounts. In ornate but tidy writing, there was a list of paired names. Each pair followed by a figure, a date, and a brief note. Many of the notes read '*priv. res.*', but some had different entries such as '*Add's*' or what looks like the name of a house.

'Do you know these places?' Vita asked.

'*Add's* is presumably Addenbrooke's hospital,' Jane said. 'The other names are not familiar. The earliest dates are nearly twenty years ago. This first one is *January 12th 1887. Lady Celia Lampton. James Lampton, 28. 100 guineas. Lampton Manor.*'

They glanced at one another before Jane reached down and flipped the pages to the most recent entry. It read *Lady Celia Lampton, Agnes Palmer, 77. 50 guineas. Bulman's, Halsey.'*

'Agnes Palmer is the old lady Miss Bulman told us about,' Jane said. 'Gerald was right. This ledger seems to be a list of the patients Potter has done away with.'

'What does '*stipend*' mean? Look, it appears several times,' Vita wondered.

'Vita! There are pages of names!' Jane said. She turned the neat pages of the ledger. 'There must be more than forty!'

'*Stipend* always appears beside a titled name, look,' Vita pointed out half a dozen entries.

'A regular payment? Perhaps these are wealthier clients who pay a regular fee as a retainer and call Potter in to dispose of people whenever it suits them,' Jane said calmly.

'Surely not!' Vita was appalled. 'That would amount to murder on demand. If that's what Potter offered, Jane, why would anybody be mad enough to write everything down? This ledger is the most damning evidence there could ever be!'

'Miss Finch likes things tidy, as Gerald said in his letter.'

'But why, if she had kept meticulous secret records for nearly twenty years, has she been so careless now?'

'Perhaps their well-organised system is failing. Or Potter's drunkenness is making him reckless,' Jane said. She looked again at the ledger, turning the pages, reading the names. 'They charged much less in some cases than in others. I wonder why? Servants are cheaper to dispose of than members of the aristocracy, perhaps?' She shuddered. 'It makes my flesh crawl.'

'Perhaps Potter is drinking to drown his guilty

conscience? But we are rushing to conclusions. We can't be sure that any of this is true.'

The lights in the carriage suddenly dimmed and then re-lit. The brakes squealed, and the train pulled into Waterfen station.

CHAPTER 22

Snowflakes danced in the platform lights. Vita recognised the crossing keeper's cottage and imagined Bob Marshall standing ready at the gates, still oblivious to the cold.

A carriage door slammed further down the train. The women looked at each other across the empty carriage. Vita closed the ledger, wrapped it hastily back in her shawl, and clasped it on her knee.

In a rush of freezing air, the door of their carriage was thrown back. The closely wrapped figure of a woman climbed in. She wore a dark grey coat with the hood high, and a veiled hat, black lacework hiding her face. She slammed the door closed behind her and stood looking away, out of the window.

Jane and Vita shrank further back into their seats. Vita gripped the ledger tightly.

Turning on her heel, the new passenger stepped without warning towards Jane and Vita. 'I will take that, please. It belongs to me,' she declared. Her voice was shrill and her movements jerky. 'Hand it to me now and no more will be said. Give it to me or I shall take it by force.'

Neither of the young women spoke. The situation was so extraordinary that it seemed unreal. It was difficult to take seriously a threat from a slight woman who seemed about twice their age, however fiercely she spoke. The train juddered into motion and she had to cling to a luggage rack to keep her balance.

'You are Miss Finch, I believe,' Vita said, hoping to distract her.

'That is none of your concern. Hand me that ledger. It is mine. You have no right to take it. It is stolen property.'

Both young women looked silently back. Vita now holding the ledger firmly to her chest.

'Miss Finch,' Jane said. 'I'm sure there has been a misunderstanding…'

The older woman turned slowly to Jane. As she did, Vita saw her slide a knife from her pocket. To her horror, Vita recognised it as a medical scalpel. She held the blade towards Jane first, then turned and aimed it at Vita.

'You imagine, don't you, that I would not have the courage to use this? I will cut your pretty faces to shreds if you don't hand that book you have stolen back to me immediately. You are nothing but a pair of dirty thieves.'

'And we believe that you, Miss Finch, are an accessory to murder,' Jane spoke calmly, but Miss Finch responded with a twist and a lunge of the knife.

Vita saw only a brief movement, a flicker of the grey fabric of Miss Finch's coat, but she heard a shriek of shock and fear from Jane. When Miss Finch stood upright again, Jane was clutching her neck with both hands. Blood was already showing on her gloves.

The sight seemed to shock the attacker, too. Enough for her to take a step back and look in surprise at her own weapon. Her eye then turned to Vita and the ledger. She lunged to grab it; the blade passing dangerously close to Vita's neck. With only one hand free, Miss Finch tried ineffectually to yank the book out of Vita's grasp. Vita hung on. Miss Finch grunted and stepped back. She dropped the scalpel and grabbed the book with both hands, hauling at it with every bit of the strength her righteous fury allowed. It was still tangled in the shawl, making it slip out of her grasp and sending her reeling backwards.

Vita looked across at Jane and saw her looking in shock at the blood on her own hand. 'Jane, has she hurt you?'

Jane looked across, her eyes wide.

'*Give me that ledger!*' The shriek was so loud that for a moment it drowned the roar of the train. Miss Finch threw herself bodily towards Vita, who slid the ledger out of the shawl and onto the seat before sitting on it. It wasn't graceful, but she hoped the barrier of her whole body might stop Miss Finch.

It did no such thing. Miss Finch reached for Vita's hat, hauled it off her head and grabbed her hair with both hands, twisting and tugging. The pain made Vita yell. She reached forward, but it was difficult to grab Miss Finch's arms through the thick wool fabric of her coat. Vita could only pull the fabric this way and that to unbalance her attacker.

They felt the train slow as it approached Cambridge.

With a vicious tug, Miss Finch hauled Vita out of her seat by the hair, but Vita kicked as she slid to the floor of the carriage, her boots pounding against Miss Finch's ankles. This brought her attacker to her knees, losing her grip. Both Jane and Vita grabbed again for the ledger. Jane reached it first and held it aloft, stepping over Miss Finch. Jane wrapped her cape over the ledger and turned her back, preparing to leap out as soon as the train stopped at Cambridge station.

Miss Finch was on her hands and knees, head down, panting with the exertion, but as they drew in to the platform at Cambridge and the lights of the station shone into the carriage, she suddenly threw back her head and screamed piercingly. 'Help! Police! Help! I am being attacked! Stop thief! Stop thief! Somebody help me!'

Heads turned along the platform. Hearing the screams, several men waiting for the train ran alongside, others fell back in alarm. A police officer ran forward, pulling a whistle from his pocket. Guards and station attendants pressed closer. By the time the train shuddered to a halt, several uniformed men were ready to throw back the door.

'Where's the thief, Miss? Is he here? Are you hurt?' A guard spoke to Jane from the platform.

'I am wounded, please, I need...' but even as she said this, her knees buckled and she fell into the arms of the nearest bystander. Two uniformed men leapt into the carriage.

'Help! Help me!' Miss Finch kept up her shouts. 'They have thrown me down. They have taken my purse! I thought they would kill me!'

The guard looked in surprise at Vita, and then back at Miss Finch. 'I've got this one, Sergeant. You come here with me, young lady.' He plunged past Miss Finch and grabbed Vita by the arm, twisting her elbow behind her.

'But I...'

'She knocked me down! She tried to steal my purse! She threatened me with a knife!' Miss Finch cried, as a pair of guards helped her to her feet. 'I thought I should be murdered.'

'Was it this woman, Madam? Was it her, your attacker?'

'It was both of them. They were together. They have

stolen my purse and an important ledger. It belongs to me. They snatched it from me.'

'Is this true?' demanded the constable, his face reddening at the terrible thought of violent young women thieving from innocent passengers. A crowd had gathered on the platform outside the carriage door. People craned their necks hoping to glimpse the villains and their poor, defenceless lady victim.

'No, it is not true,' Vita told him. 'Not in the least! She attacked *us*. She changed carriage at Waterfen and attacked us!'

'She says you were trying to take her purse,' the constable said, severely.

'That's a lie!'

'Do I need to detain the train?' the station master called from behind the nosy crowd.

'No need,' called the guard. 'We're disembarking the suspects now.'

The onlookers stared angrily as the police officer led Vita away.

CHAPTER 23

*J*nspector Llewellyn's office at the police station was small. It smelt of furniture polish, damp wool and something that might have been gravy. A shelf behind his desk held a row of impressive sporting trophies awarded by the Inter-Counties Constabulary Sporting Association, and one wall was covered with group photographs of the Police Officers of Cambridge standing proudly at attention in tiered and helmeted rows.

With the fire roaring, three ladies and a sergeant on the other side of the desk, the rising temperature of the room soon added to the tension.

Several minutes had already passed with the women making counter accusations. The older one in particular was difficult to stop. The Inspector's patience was wearing thin. Of the two young ladies, one was dishevelled - her hair a tangled orange bird's nest and her spectacles bent out of shape and the other wore a police first aider's large bandage around her neck and the side of her face, but was still (he could not help but notice) of a delicate beauty rarely observed in a police station. These were clearly not the usual sort of railway hoodlums.

The Inspector thought with brief longing of his dinner of mutton chops, mashed potatoes and gravy. Hastily concealed in his desk drawer, its meaty aroma still reached his nostrils, even as it congealed. He looked down at the blue covered ledger that lay open on the desk before him. In his brief examination of it, he could see nothing that the most law-abiding doctor might not have written. Names, addresses, next of kin, dates, fees. There were, perhaps, one or two oddities, but as evidence of criminal activity, it seemed to offer very little.

'Inspector, you must have Dr Potter arrested. We don't know where he is, he may present a danger…'

'It is perfectly clear from these entries that he is capable of …'

'That ledger is the property of my employer! They have no right to it. These accusations are absurd! Absurd!'

The older lady in the veiled hat attempted to snatch the ledger from Llewellyn's desk. Llewellyn was known for his patience, but such disrespect was too much, even for him. He placed a heavy hand on it and stood, revealing his full six feet four inches of barrel-chested authority.

'Sergeant,' he said, quietly. 'Remove all three of these ladies immediately. Take them to the basement. I shall interview them one at a time.'

The older lady was still protesting at the top of her voice as the sergeant and two constables conducted her away.

It was rare, Llewellyn thought, as he slid his dinner out of the drawer and tucked his napkin back into his collar, for a victim to be so much louder and more disagreeable than her assailants. Rare, but not unknown.

CHAPTER 24

*T*he basement of Cambridge police station in Regent's Street had six barred and locked cells, but only two small rooms that might be used for interviews. The sergeant did not like ladies in cells. Besides, a chorus of shouts reminded him that most were already occupied by the boisterously drunk and disorderly.

On the way down, he observed that the two younger women seemed the least troublesome, so he put them in Room Two, which while not a cell, was bolted on the outside and had only a half-window.

The older lady threatened the Sergeant all the way downstairs with her Member of Parliament, her uncle (a judge, she claimed), her employer (a distinguished medical man) and his patients - all powerful members of the aristocracy, by the sound of it. This lady he put in Room Three, a smaller, darker room, which also bolted on the outside, and which, while well lit, had no window at all.

Her shrieks of outrage were still ringing in his ears as he climbed back up to Inspector Llewellyn's office. The smell of chops was still evident, but all other signs of dinner had now been removed.

'Have a look at this, Sergeant, and tell me what you make of it.' Llewellyn pushed the ledger over his desk. It was open, and the Sergeant read a few lines, running a finger along and frowning as he did so.

'Seems to be names, Sir. Names of patients, I suppose. And dates. And fees.'

'High fees, wouldn't you say?'

'I would, Sir, but perhaps these are the wealthy sort.'

'The wealthy sort, in my experience, rarely overpay their doctors or anyone else who renders them a service,' Llewellyn said.

'Why would they pay so much, then?'

'Those dates, I reckon, are dates they were certified dead. Certified by Potter himself. That would be easy to verify.'

'He could kill them and certify himself that they died of natural causes?'

'He could.'

The Sergeant gave a low whistle. 'There are an awful lot of names here, Sir,' he said, straightening up.

'Yes. And all of them wealthy and powerful people. If any of this is true, it will be enough to keep the cleverest lawyers of Cambridge - and of London, I shouldn't wonder - busy with Potter's case for years.' The Inspector paused and sighed as if anticipating the long struggle ahead. 'These are not the sort of people who give in easily. Put it in the safe, Sergeant. I wouldn't like to think of any of those ladies making off with this ledger, but on its own, it won't be enough. Meanwhile, I shall start by interviewing one of the quieter ones. The shouter, the older lady with the scar, will give me indigestion. I'll tackle her last.'

As the Sergeant rounded a corner of the stairs, he almost

fell over yet another lady - this one at least not shrieking, injured or dishevelled - hurrying up towards the Inspector's office.

'Ah, Sergeant,' she said, 'I must see Inspector Llewellyn immediately. It is a matter of the greatest urgency.'

The Sergeant was doubtful, but the lady showed him a letter, waving it before him for emphasis. 'I know the Inspector. He will want to see this, Sergeant. People's lives are at risk.'

Her tone was impressively commanding. The sergeant later told his wife that it put him in mind of the late Queen herself. As she stepped into Llewellyn's office he heard her say, 'Inspector, I have a letter you will certainly want to see, and - I do hope you don't mind - I took the liberty of bringing an apple pie my chef has just baked.'

A proper lady, the sergeant concluded.

CHAPTER 25

'However did you do it, Mrs Brocklehurst?' Jane asked, as they took off their coats in the hall of 144 Eden Street. 'Vita and I thought we were there for the night at the very least.'

Aunt Louisa removed her fur hat and gloves and patted her hair into shape in the mirror.

'I simply showed Llewellyn the letter, exactly according to your instructions. You were not back by six o'clock, so I did as you asked,' she said with a quiet smile. She was pleased to be credited with obtaining the young women's release. 'Taking an apple pie was a good decision too, I must admit.'

Tabitha appeared and was sent to make tea, 'and bring the sherry, Tabitha,' Aunt Louisa added.

She brushed a little dust from her skirt and led them into the warm sitting room, where the chairs were already set around the fire. 'Now before we settle down, Vita, please go over to Dr Goodman and ask him to come and look at Miss Douglas's injury.'

'Oh, there is no need, really,' Jane said. 'She only caught me with the tip of the blade. It is only a matter of a tiny cut.'

But Aunt Louisa insisted. Goodman dressed two cuts, one on Jane's neck, the other on the point of her jaw.

'Her aim was poor,' he remarked, 'but she was in the right general area to reach an artery and do irreparable damage to your face. You were lucky.' Accepting a sherry, he joined them beside the fire as the young women explained the afternoon's events, including the struggle over the ledger on the train and their arrest.

'A successful day,' Goodman said, 'but as your medical adviser, I must counsel you not to engage in brawling in a public place in future, particularly not with an armed attacker. The injuries may not be so slight another time.'

'I imagine the police will be searching for Dr Potter even now,' Aunt Louisa said. 'We have no way of knowing whether he is really guilty of the crimes Dr Linn suspected, of course.'

'The ledger did seem to confirm it,' Jane said, 'each entry apparently recorded the death of a patient and the sum of money paid.'

'But looked at another way, it could simply be the sum of money they paid for the unfortunate patient's treatment, as Inspector Llewellyn pointed out,' Aunt Louisa said.

'On its own, the ledger is probably not enough, but together with the letter…?' Vita began.

'… and we shouldn't forget the medicines Potter ordered from Gadd's. I told Llewellyn it was in the Left Luggage office at the station. That might add to the case,' Jane put in.

'But Dr Linn recovering his memory would be the best evidence, I suppose,' said Aunt Louisa. 'Can we be confident he will recover it?'

'Not completely confident, no,' Goodman said. 'And clever lawyers would ridicule the evidence of a witness who has suffered amnesia, I imagine.'

GOODMAN SWALLOWED the last of his sherry and set the glass down. 'I find it difficult to believe that - I hardly even know what to call it - euthanasia; mercy killing; or simply murder, could be carried out on such a scale. One hears of the occasional case. Medicine has few remedies for some of the dreadful suffering doctors have to witness. Every doctor has been driven to consider...'

He did not finish the sentence, but only sighed and looked into the fire for a moment. 'But it seems to me that what that ledger records and what Dr Linn discovered is a systematic policy of murder on request. And on a considerable scale. I find it very hard to believe that any medical man could stray so far.'

Jane changed the subject. 'Have you seen Dr Linn today, Dr Goodman? How is he?'

Goodman was glad to speak of something else. 'Only briefly. He is much as before. He reported no new memories but his other injuries are healing well. Did I mention that my colleague and I believe he was drugged? That might partially explain his loss of memory, but not for such a long time. It seems likely that he hit his head and was badly concussed when he was thrown down the well.'

'The sooner that man Potter is under lock and key, the better,' Aunt Louisa remarked. 'He seems both ruthless and out of control. If he has taken to the drink, he surely presents even more of a risk.'

'We should not scare ourselves,' Goodman said. 'I know Llewellyn. He is not one to rush into action, but I believe he is an effective officer of the law. Now Ladies, I shall leave you to lock your doors and get a good night's sleep. There is nothing more to be done tonight, at any rate.'

CHAPTER 26

*B*y ten o'clock, all the ladies had retired to bed. Jane in the spare room because nobody would think of allowing her to walk back to her nurse's residence in the dark and snow, and besides, Aunt Louisa had promised both Dr Goodman and Inspector Llewellyn to keep her under observation. Such is the level of care devoted to a lovely young woman whose face has been injured, even slightly.

By half-past eleven, however, Vita was back in the sitting room with *Atkins' Pure Mathematics* on her lap, trying to work out the calculation on page 85 before the embers of the fire. Whether it was the excitement of the day, she couldn't tell, but the thoughts refused to stop racing in her mind, so she had given up and was trying algebra as a distraction. This was not a successful plan, and she was wondering whether to read something else when the door opened quietly and Jane slipped into the room. She sat opposite Vita, pulling her borrowed dressing gown around her.

'You couldn't sleep either, Vita?' Jane said.

'Do you think they will keep Miss Finch in a cell?' Vita asked. 'Imagine how she will complain about that!'

'I doubt they will. She will deny everything. She is probably at liberty by now.'

Both looked at the glowing embers for a while.

'I am concerned that nobody knows Dr Potter's whereabouts,' Jane said.

'The police will arrest him quickly on the evidence of the ledger and Dr Linn's letter together, surely.'

'They will not rush to arrest a professional man, you know. They dread making an error or a false arrest of someone like a doctor. The consequences would be serious for someone like Llewellyn.'

'They would be equally serious if he did *not* carry out his duty.'

Jane turned from the fire - the glow of it still lighting her features. 'Vita, you don't think he would try to reach Gerald in the hospital, do you? I have been lying upstairs imagining how easy it might be for Potter - a doctor, and presumably a familiar face at the hospital - to slip into the ward.'

Vita looked back. 'I was imagining the same thing,' she admitted.

Both looked again into the embers.

'And, Vita, if Potter has already killed several people - which is what the ledger seemed to show - why should he have any qualms about killing again? Especially if it would save his own skin.'

'He might try a second time to dispose of Dr Linn, you mean? Surely he would not risk that?'

'In his right mind, perhaps not, but Dr Potter is not in his right mind, is he? He is a drinker and his situation is desperate. He is probably not capable of calculating the risk he is running. He is at large, and there is every reason to believe he is dangerous.'

In the silence that fell as they both considered this, they

heard steady footsteps approach in the street outside. Vita went to the window and peered around the curtain. 'It is only Constable Williamson on his beat,' she said. 'We know him. He is walking out with our maid, Tabitha.'

A thought struck her.

'I could ask him whether Potter has been arrested. He might know.'

Jane took her place at the window as Vita hurried downstairs and out of the door, grabbing her coat as she passed the hall stand. Jane watched as Vita caught the constable up under a street lamp. A light but steady snow fell, the flakes swirling in the streetlights like feathery dancers in the spotlight of an aerial ballet. The two figures' breath clouded around them as they spoke. Jane saw Vita turn and hurry back.

'They will certainly not arrest him tonight,' Vita said, breathless and bringing a gust of cold air into the room with her.

'But why not?' Jane asked.

'They plan to send someone to Halsey tomorrow. It's Christmas. Many of the officers are on leave and at home with their families, he said.'

'Oh Vita! That is not enough. Gerald could be in danger!'

'I asked if they had sent officers to the hospital,' Vita said.

'And had they?'

'No. There were not enough to spare. Besides, they are not aware of any threat.'

Jane stood and made to leave the room. 'I shall go to the hospital myself,' she said.

'And I will come with you. If nothing happens, we will lose only a night's sleep. If Potter does come…'

'What shall we do if he comes?' Jane asked, with her hand on the door.

'Blow the whistle, of course!' Vita told her. Both hurried to dress. They left within minutes and were at the hospital soon after midnight.

CHAPTER 27

*H*ow different a familiar building looks at night. Even the most functional and well-lit halls and passageways, well-known and unremarkable in the daytime, become shadowy and develop mysterious corners in the dark. Their gloomy emptiness distorts them. Sounds misbehave. In a passageway fading into the invisible distance, the echo of a door closing or a fleeting snatch of conversation lose all proportion.

The hospital's main entrance was closed, but they saw a nurse in her long cloak leave through a side door and had no difficulty entering there. The long hallway inside was deserted.

'We should not attract attention if we look unhurried and purposeful,' Jane said. 'We might be nurses or housekeeping staff.'

Their plan, agreed as they hurried through snowy streets to the hospital, was that Jane would keep watch in the patient's room. She was a visitor known to the staff, so nobody should be alarmed, and if they asked questions about such a late visit, she would mention Dr Goodman's name and hope that would be sufficient.

Vita would sit in the long second-floor corridor outside the ward, where there was a row of chairs near the staircase. Nobody could reach the ward without her seeing and she would have time to raise the alarm if Dr Potter came near. She had the whistle in her pocket for the purpose.

She only realised after she had taken her place that she did not know what Dr Potter looked like. She pondered this as she drew her coat around her and settled in for a night's guard duty. Potter was old enough to have been at Halsey for about twenty years, so he must be at least forty-five. She had a remarkably developed idea of what Dr Potter looked like, but on examination she found that this was based on nothing but imagination. She had pictured a country doctor willing to dispatch inconvenient relatives and dependents as a favour to his circle of wealthy connections, and she had done so convincingly - at least to herself. In her mind, he was red-faced and round. He wore rough tweeds and a country-man's boots and carried a scuffed and battered doctor's bag of black leather. Above all, a man capable of such evil had a side-long way of looking and eyes as cold as a codfish on a slab.

But on rational re-consideration, there in a gloomy corridor, Vita had to admit that all this was nothing but shamefully foolish prejudice.

The chilly corridor smelled of floor polish and carbolic. A low hum, a sort of buzz of occupation and distant activity was all Vita heard for long interludes. Now and then footsteps on the stairs or the distant rattle of a trolley several corridors away reached her. A pair of nurses deep in quiet conversation, passed once, but nothing more. Somewhere outside, a church bell sounded the quarter hour. Vita wondered if it was still snowing and whether the snow was falling on her father's vicarage in Devon. She wondered how her father was managing, now that she and her brother were both in Cambridge. The parish was remote; people were scattered. Visiting meant long rides over the moors. He would be busy, but well fed at Christmas by the generous ladies of the parish. She wondered when she would see him again.

The man was close before she noticed. He was tall and came towards her with the long stride of an athlete. In a top hat and a greatcoat which swept around him, he seemed at first to make no sound. As he drew nearer, she could still not hear footsteps. Instead, a slight rhythmic squeak kept pace. It was the sound of gym shoes on a wooden gymnasium floor. His shoes had soft soles.

Vita's picture of a gingery tweed-wearing Potter evaporated and was replaced by this lean and energetic man. He passed her with no sign of noticing, then paused and pulled off his coat, setting it with the top hat, which he brushed the snow from, on a chair a little further along the hall. He then turned abruptly and passed through the ward doors, leaving them bouncing behind him.

But was it Potter?

Vita, so certain before, now found herself in doubt. He might be a visitor - someone whose father or brother was in the ward. He might be a surgeon called in an emergency.

Dr Linn's was one of two private rooms on the left, just inside the ward's high double doors. Vita reasoned that Potter - if this man was Potter - would not know which room to go to. Potter might assume Linn was in the main ward, which was a long, high-ceilinged room with twenty-four beds on each side. It would take some time to identify an intended victim among so many sleeping patients. Explanations would be needed. Night nurses were in attendance at their station in the centre of the ward. This should allow enough time for

Vita to slip into Dr Linn's room and warn Jane and the patient.

But no. As she watched the newcomer through the glass panel of the ward's double doors, she could see him peering through the window in the door of the single room next to Dr Linn's.

He stepped back and looked towards the main body of the ward separated from this lobby area by another pair of double doors. There was no movement from the ward.

Vita ducked, in case he looked in her direction, her pulse pounding, then peered through the glass again. As she watched, the man slid a hand into his pocket. He drew out what looked like a silver cigar box, but when he flipped the lid of it open, what he removed was a silver and glass syringe. He checked it, holding it briefly to the light to examine the contents, then slid it up into his left sleeve and moved toward the next door.

'May I ask what you are doing here?' a voice at her shoulder made Vita start. The whistle she had been pulling from her pocket clattered to the floor between them.

'He is... this man... I believe that man means harm to one of your patients!' Vita gasped.

The woman wore the black uniform dress and elaborate starched bonnet of a senior nurse. She looked at Vita sternly. 'Can you explain more?' she asked.

'I have good reason to believe that man might attack Dr Linn, the amnesiac patient in the side room. Please, we must stop him.'

Both looked again through the glass panel. The man carrying the syringe had heard something. He looked their way.

The senior nurse threw the doors open and stepped inside. 'May I help you?' she asked.

Vita followed. The man assessed the two women calmly. 'Matron. Perhaps you can advise. I have called to see my colleague, Dr Gerald Linn,' he said. 'I have only just learnt of his accident. I came immediately.'

'If you come with me, I shall find a nurse to accompany you, Doctor Potter,' the matron said.

She recognises him! Vita thought.

'That won't be necessary,' Potter said, 'if you could just show me to him. It will only be a brief visit.'

'I would prefer a nurse to be present, Doctor. That is our normal practice, as you know. I will accompany you myself if you would prefer.'

The matron, an angular woman, hawk-nosed and of regal bearing, now stood between Dr Potter and the door of Dr Linn's room. She smiled mildly, but nobody could have doubted her authority. Potter, knowing he had no choice, nodded in acceptance. A flush of colour altered his face.

The matron put her hand on the door and as she opened it, caught Vita's eye with a silent order to follow.

As they entered the dim room, Jane started from the chair beside the bed. The patient slept on.

'We are quite a crowd in here. I see,' said the matron, lowering her voice, 'that Dr Linn already has a visitor.' She looked with disapproval at Jane, not knowing how she came to be there.

Dr Potter went to the foot of the bed and took up the clip-board of medical notes.

'He is your colleague, you say?' the matron asked him.

'Yes. Poor fellow,' Potter said. 'Heaven only knows how he came to be in this condition.'

'A brutal attack is the police's conclusion,' Jane said. She spoke with barely disguised anger. Potter gave her a long, irritable glance.

'I have many times seen injuries such as this from an accident. After all, he was found near the railway line,' Potter said. He approached the head of the bed. 'Only last year I treated a young man who had stumbled out of the door of a moving a train.'

Jane drew closer to the bed herself. The patient slept on.

Potter leaned over the pillows to examine the injuries to Linn's face. Vita watched with sickening anxiety as he moved his left hand, with the syringe hidden just inside the cuff, towards the patient's neck.

He surely would not attempt anything with all of us here, she thought, *not with us watching.*

Potter straightened suddenly and stepped back. 'Well, Matron, he is obviously in the best of hands. I am relieved to see my colleague so well attended. Thank you for allowing me to see him.'

'Not at all, Dr Potter,' the matron said. She followed him out of the room.

Jane and Vita looked at each other and then sighed in relief.

'He is carrying a syringe,' Vita said. 'He has it in his sleeve.'

The look of horror was still on Jane's face as the matron returned.

'Doctor Potter is a regular visitor to patients at this hospital. You have made serious allegations against him,' she told Vita. 'And you,' she looked at Jane, 'have no business being here at his bedside unsupervised overnight. It is against all usual practice. I would advise you both to leave unless you can provide me with an extremely good explanation.'

Both Jane and Vita launched into summaries of the past day's events. The senior nurse took a step backwards, holding up a hand for silence.

'One at a time. You have two minutes. I am interrupting my night's rounds, and there are several more wards and many more patients waiting to be seen.'

'We have evidence,' Jane said, 'that Doctor Potter has been taking money in return for euthanising certain patients. He seems to have been doing so for many years.'

'There is a documentary proof with the police and they intend to arrest Doctor Potter soon,' Vita added.

'I cannot act on accusations of this sort,' said the matron, 'certain people are quick to make allegations against doctors.'

'Dr Linn found evidence of Dr Potter's actions and immediately afterwards he went missing. Then he was found injured and with no memory. We believe Potter came here to silence Dr Linn. We told the police.'

'Why did the police not arrest him?'

'They have too few officers on duty over the Christmas holiday,' Vita said.

'Well, I sympathise with them there, but I cannot act on the basis of such wild ideas,' said the matron. 'Dr Potter is well known. He is a regular visitor to patients here.'

'Matron, he is carrying a syringe. I saw him put it up his sleeve!' Vita said.

'He is a doctor. Carrying a syringe would not be unusual, I daresay.'

'We have good reason to believe he plans to kill Dr Linn,' Jane said. 'He knows what Potter has done. Potter may even have been responsible for the attack that brought Dr Linn here.'

CHAPTER 28

*T*he matron's light blue eyes flicked between Jane and Vita. 'This is a little far-fetched for my tastes. Even so,' she said, 'if you insist on staying here, I shall not object, as long as you do not interrupt the usual work of the nurses.'

'Thank you, Matron,' Jane said.

Her words were hardly out before footsteps rang out along the corridor outside the ward.

'This is the one, Ward Two,' a voice said, and two police officers threw back the double doors. Between them, a shabby man in a patched tweed jacket was held on either side by an arm.

'Good heavens, what next,' the matron said, turning the full force of her authority on this odd group of visitors. 'Sergeant Dunwoody, what is the meaning of invading my ward in this manner?'

The sergeant, who held the man's left arm, was a head and shoulders taller than the matron, but that didn't stop him looking like a schoolboy caught with a catapult. 'My apologies, Matron, but this man is a suspect in Dr Linn's case. We want him to identify this patient.'

'And it cannot wait until morning?'

'I'm afraid not, Matron, given the fact that a murderer might be at large.'

The matron took this in with only a long blink to betray her rapid reconsideration of the situation. 'Bring him into Dr Linn's room,' she said, 'but please try not to wake the rest of the ward.'

As soon as the man saw Dr Linn, he hung his head. 'That's him. I never looked close, but I reckon that's the one,' he said. 'Is he hurt bad?'

Vita and Jane had slipped into the room behind the men. Jane said, 'He is lucky to be alive. What do you know? What happened to him?'

'Now, Miss, this is police business…' the sergeant said, but the man was staring at the patient and wanted to answer Jane's question.

'It was me. I… I pushed him down.'

'Down? Down where?'

'Down the old well by Merrily Farm.'

'You threw him into a well? Why?'

The police officer stepped between Jane and the prisoner. 'This isn't the time or place, Miss. We have accused him of attacking this man. That is all you need to know. Now that he has identified the victim, he should go back in the cells.'

'But why? Why would you do such a terrible thing?' Jane asked, ignoring the policeman.

'He gave me money. My wife's sick. The cattle have had the fever. I needed it.'

'Who? Who gave you money?'

'I don't know him. He was just a well-dressed gentleman. It was in a pub.'

'That'll do,' said the police sergeant, trying to shift the man out of the room. But the prisoner was not so easily stopped. 'Look,' he said, 'I know I did wrong. A stranger - a man I'd never seen before came up to me in the pub and asked me if I ever had to bury a dead beast, and I said yes, I did. And he said, if I give you ten guineas, would you bury one for me? Ten guineas! That pays my rent. I said yes. Only it wasn't a beast. I met him in the lane by Rook's End and he had something on his cart under a cover. I took it for a sheep or a calf. But when I got to the farm and looked, it wasn't a sheep, it was a man. I thought he was dead, but I never looked too close. I thought I should hang for it. I didn't know what to do. I thought to put him on the railway line, so he'd be - so the train would hit him, and it would seem like an accident. Only I couldn't do it. I didn't have the heart to do it. In the end I put him in the old well.'

Those gathering in the room all looked at the man, appalled. There was no stopping him now. 'But I couldn't sleep. I kept thinking of him down there at the bottom of that old well. I went back to look. Took a lantern and leaned over, but he was gone. Nothing there, only some shoes at the bottom.'

The onlookers collectively flinched at this.

'He must have dropped them when he climbed out. I don't know how. Not one man in a thousand could climb out of a place like that. Not without a rope or a ladder. Gave me a fright.'

'And would these be the shoes? The ones you're wearing now?' The police officer asked.

The man looked away. 'I saw them down there. Good shoes. I couldn't see the harm in using them.'

'That's enough from you, now,' the police officer said. 'You're coming back to the station with me, my lad.'

'Wait!' A voice from the bed made everyone start. Everyone turned to see the patient struggling to sit up. 'I heard what this man said.'

'Dr Linn, you shouldn't be troubled with this now,' the matron told him, stepping forward and lifting his wrist to take his pulse, as if by reflex.

'I am not troubled. I remember nothing of this. He might have left me on the railway line, but he did not do so. I would like to thank him for that.' He turned to the farmer, who was now hanging his head as the two policemen held him up. 'Thank you, Sir. What you did was wrong, but you were desperate and your wife is sick.'

Both police officers looked closely at their prisoner to check his reaction, but the man was rendered silent.

'How did you find this man?' Vita asked in the pause.

Sergeant Dunwoody looked pleased. 'Tranter, from the shoe shop. He saw a pair of his fancy shoes walking about on an old farmer's feet.' He pointed downwards. Protruding from the prisoner's worn, frayed and dirt-hardened workmen's trousers, were a muddied pair of the finest brown brogues. 'He made the mistake of wearing them to market.'

'I should like those shoes back when it is convenient,' Dr Linn remarked from his pillows.

'I could take them for you now, Sir. It's chilly out for walking to the station in bare feet, but I daresay this man could put up with a little discomfort,' Dunwoody offered.

'No. Let him wear them back to the cells. He might have thrown me on the railway line - he meant to show mercy.'

The matron started, looked sharply at the little watch she had pinned to her white apron, and left to continue her rounds, saying only, 'Well, I never!'

CHAPTER 29

*T*he night rooms for on-call doctors were on the top floor. They were small bedrooms with the barest furnishings, for the use of junior doctors who were on call for twenty-four hours at a time.

Potter closed the door behind him. 'There is nobody at this end of the corridor,' he said, 'but keep your voice down, all the same.'

'You are sober,' Miss Finch said. She was sitting rigidly on the small chair at the foot of the bed.

'You seem surprised.'

'Well,' she said, 'it is rare enough.'

'I drink because of the dreary sameness of Halsey. This is much more interesting!'

'*Interesting*, you call it?'

'Come, Edith, we both yearned for excitement,' he said. 'We both wanted to escape the small-minded people of Halsey.'

'I was nearly jailed this afternoon!'

'You exaggerate, surely.'

'I was in the cells at the police station! There are charges pending against me!'

'But they let you go. You were not there because of...' he paused, with a vague gesture of his hand, '... all we have done, over the years.'

'All *you* have done.'

'Oh come, Edith. You know you are as guilty as I.'

'You are the killer.'

'And you, the killer's co-conspirator. It is just as grave a charge. We shall both hang, if the local dim-wits ever work it all out, which was not likely until recently.' Potter walked to the window, turning his back on her. He drummed his fingers against the glass, then turned towards her. 'Did I know about the ledger, by the way? Had you mentioned that you wrote everything down in your best handwriting? All the details in one place, so that anyone with the wit to see it could tell exactly how we had amassed our little fortune over the years? Had you mentioned that to me Edith, because if you did, I must have forgotten.'

Edith Finch clenched her jaw. Her face grew pale, making the jagged scar appear darker. 'Somebody needed to be well-organised,' she hissed. She did not look at him. 'You were not capable yourself.'

'And that suited you very well.'

He bent and said these words into her face.

A silence fell in the chilly room. Snow was now falling steadily and settling on the rooftops that they could see out of the window. 'Edith, my dear, we need not fall out at this late stage. There is still work to be done.'

'You are quite mad,' she told him quietly. 'You have been deranged for years.'

'And you, Edith? You would consider yourself sane? You,

who kept my books and banked the money I earned by ending lives?'

'I have always been a tidy administrator since I kept the parish records for my father.' She said this with a note of pride.

'You stole from him relentlessly.'

Miss Finch ran a finger over the starched white apron she was wearing, ignoring that remark for several minutes. Then, sinking a little in her chair, she said, 'He counted my hairpins. My stockings were so darned that you could not see the original weave. He once fed me bread and cheese at every meal for four months. I still want to break something whenever I think of that man.'

'I have always assumed that you stole from me, too. Your light fingers nimbly tidying little sums into your own accounts here and there.' He waved his fingers at her, like someone preparing to sit at the piano. 'Come now, Edith, I know I'm right. It does not worry me. I quite admired your barefaced lying; your fraud; your small deceptions; your petty embezzlements. We both knew what was going on.'

'Oh, but you didn't know,' she hissed. 'You were too busy swallowing whisky to know. Or dallying your afternoons away with the landlady at the Valiant Trooper.'

'Ah, so you knew about that?'

'I know it all. I know people. They tell me.'

'But you have no friends, Edith. Nobody likes you, or trusts you.'

'That is of no concern. My only concern has been to save enough to go away. A new life. I have all I need now.'

'Congratulations! And where are you headed, Edith? Where is your new life to be? Or perhaps it is a secret.'

'New York!' she said. As she pronounced it, her features

softened and warmed. The name of the city alone kindled a flame of hope inside her.

'New York! My, my, you are ambitious!' Potter said, turning his back and looking out of the window again.

'All I need is to reach Southampton. I know the sailings. I can secure my passage easily.'

'Why haven't you gone already?'

She looked confused at this, frowning and looking up at his back. 'Those wretched girls. The ledger. And Linn.'

'They are in Linn's room, both of them, by the way,' Potter said.

'Who are they?'

'Who knows? His sisters, his mistresses? It hardly matters. I have what I need to get past a pair of girls.'

'You will kill them?'

'They are not worth the trouble.'

'But Linn. You still plan to kill Linn? I can help. I wore my nurse's uniform.'

'Linn must go. I read his notes. He has no memory at present, but he will probably recover it. I should have doubled the dose - I am not used to giving this new barbital hypnotic to healthy young specimens like him. But, yes, he needs to go. Convincing evidence from a doctor - even a fool like Linn - will force the blundering local police into action.

'I can get into his room.'

Potter turned to her. 'Yes. It would be easier for a nurse - or someone dressed as one. They recognise me. The Matron is everywhere.'

'Let me do it.'

'That pair of young busybodies who have appointed themselves his guardians will recognise you.'

'They'll move some time. I can watch for the right moment.'

'He is young and healthy. It will not be easy. You will need to silence him by injecting and then - well, a nick to the artery in the neck works fast. I'm sure I can find you a scalpel.'

'I had one,' she said, 'but I must have dropped it when I cut that girl's face.'

'She's still very pretty, from what I could see, Edith. You didn't make a very good job of it.'

She sat rigid and expressionless, but a tear ran down her face.

HE TURNED TO HER AGAIN. 'Or you could just leave now, Edith. You may have to wait for the first morning train, but you can still be in Southampton by midday. With luck, you could be out of the country tomorrow.'

She blinked at him, trying to take this in, her eyes darting this way and that, as if calculating. 'What of the money?' she asked.

'Leave me enough to reach France.'

'Of course I will.'

'In the special account?'

'Yes. But I will stay and finish this. I will stop Linn telling his story first.'

'Why? Why would you do this? I am offering you the chance to get away.' Potter turned from the window to look at her. 'Why were we never lovers, Edith?' he asked.

She was looking at her hands in her lap, but her shoulders stiffened. 'This face, among other things,' she said.

'Your brute of a father did not damage it so very badly.'

'I am not lovable. If you hit a child with a coal shovel, you hurt more than her face.'

'You are not easily lovable in the ordinary way, Edith. But we are not ordinary, you and I. We might have made something of that.'

'We are too alike,' she said.

'Like twins? Yes. You have it there. But we did make something together.'

'Something. Yes.'

'We fashioned a successful practice, and a lot of money, out of unpromising raw material.'

Edith Finch smiled - a twitch across her uneven features. 'The raw material of Halsey was unpromising, certainly.'

'Take it. Take your money, Edith. Go.'

For a moment her hand reached towards him, as if to touch his arm, but he was too far away, and did not notice.

'No,' she said, 'Linn must be finished.'

Potter sighed. 'As you wish, Edith. I'll take the one in the corridor.'

CHAPTER 30

*V*ita, back in the corridor with her whistle, was making notes. Her habit of keeping a written record had been instilled by a childhood assisting her father. Together the pair had recorded bird migrations; moth numbers and varieties; the date they first heard a cuckoo each year; the date the swallows returned in the Spring; and many other of Devon's natural history events. To record her observations of scientific - and in this case even criminal - matters, came naturally. Her spectacles were crooked, bent out of shape during the struggles with Miss Finch, it was dim in the corridor and her pencil was blunt, so she was hunched over her notebook in concentration and less aware of the surroundings than might have been ideal - at least that was the only explanation she could find later for what happened.

She heard a noise - a door bang, possibly - at one end of the passageway and, turning to look, felt herself seized from the other side. A hand was over her mouth and nose. Something cold pressed into her wrist. A stab of pain; a sudden loss of strength, and she drifted away into velvety black unconsciousness, only aware, as she did so, of being lifted over a shoulder and carried away.

She awoke on a creaky bed in a small dark room she did not know. She struggled to lift her head from the pillow. Something had to be done. Something important. She needed to be somewhere, but her cloudy thoughts told her nothing more. What was she supposed to do? Who was depending on her? She could not muster the effort needed to remember. She only wanted to rest her head on the warm pillow again and sleep.

Somebody else was there. But who? In this strange dim place, that patch of greater darkness across the room was a man. A man to fear, she seemed to know. If only she could sleep a little longer, she could think about it later. Her head fell back onto the pillow again. As she closed her eyes, something forced itself insistently into her awareness. Whisky. Alert when her other senses were closing down, her sense of smell pricked her back into consciousness. Whisky? Who drank whisky? Oh yes. She remembered. It was Dr Potter.

'There, you are awake, I see,' he said from the other side of the room. 'It's cold enough in this room to freeze a junior doctor in his bed. It is a wonder any of them ever survive the night.'

'Where?' she asked. Her mouth was dry and sticky.

'Oh, just a room at Addenbrooke's. I used to sleep in places like this as a junior. Small wonder I took a little whisky now and then.'

Parts of Vita's awareness still wished she could forget this person and go back to sleep, but they were overridden by memory. Recent events began shakily to fall into place. 'Why have you brought me here?' she asked, pushing herself upright to sit and, with an awkward effort, getting her feet onto the floor. The room dipped and waved around her.

'I haven't quite decided,' he said. He took a long gulp from a hip flask, shaking it as he flipped its metal stopper back into place, checking how much was left. 'I thought I would move you out of the way and then go in and pay a visit to my colleague, poor unfortunate Doctor Linn. But when I got you here - oh, I don't know - I just couldn't summon the energy. So I stayed for a drink, and to keep you company.'

Vita wondered how much whisky he had taken, and how much it needed to render someone like Potter incapable. A lot, she guessed. More than one hip flask, at any rate. His eyes were bloodshot and his words occasionally slurred. She wanted not to be in this small space with this drunken man, but he was watchful and his chair was between her and the door.

'What do you want of me?' she asked him. Even to her cloudy brain, a few awful possibilities had already suggested themselves.

'I haven't decided that either.'

'Have you... did you hurt Jane - the woman in Dr Linn's room?'

'Jane? No. I told you I never reached there. I just brought you up here. I carried you all the way up the stairs. Two flights. Very tiring, so I felt I needed a little whisky.'

'How long ago was that?'

'Be quiet,' he said, suddenly angry. 'I'm not here to answer your questions. I won't be spoken to by some jumped up schoolgirl. Keep silent while I think.'

She noticed her notebook was on the foot of the bed. The pencil was even tucked into the page. He must have taken care to carry that, too.

~

VITA WATCHED Potter look out of the window at the snow drifting out of the sky. Large snowflakes passing the light of the window glittered like shavings of copper. The quiet of a heavy snowfall, usually so comforting, muted the still-sleeping city. That face, lifted to the window, must have been strikingly handsome once, Vita thought, but now his moustache was too black - dyed, she supposed - his eyes were puffy, his complexion mottled and flushed. He was elegantly dressed, still. A grey tailcoat suit, a narrow grey and black stripe in his trousers, his cuffs and collar spotlessly white.

'What brought you to this, Dr Potter?' she asked. She knew it was a daring question, but there was something about the look of him that suggested he was trying to decide how this strange situation should end. Engaging his thoughts could win her some time, which might be useful. Above all, she was genuinely curious. What could bring a doctor to kill? If that was really what Potter had done.

He did not reply for several minutes. The cold settled into Vita's limbs. Her coat had been left downstairs. She calculated four steps from the bed to the door, but her captor was sitting in the way, and besides, the room was still not steady about her. She was not yet certain her legs could be relied on in a dash.

'You are a young woman of the academic sort, I take it?' Potter asked, suddenly. 'I judge by your dowdy dress, your spectacles and your generally bookish demeanour.'

'I am studying at Newton College, yes,' Vita said.

'Your subject?'

'Science.'

'Indeed?' He turned to look at her curiously. 'And your aim?'

Vita did not feel like confiding her ambitions to Potter. They were new ambitions, frail and rarely spoken aloud. She hardly voiced them even to friends. He grew impatient. 'Come now, you must have some intention. Why trouble yourself with all that tedious book-bashing otherwise?'

'I should like, one day, if it is possible, if I can achieve the standard required, to qualify as a doctor,' she told him. She looked at her hands in her lap, expecting cruel laughter or cutting words, but neither came. Only more silence.

Potter eventually sighed, a long exhalation, as if something were leaving his body forever. She looked over and he - she could hardly be certain - but it looked as if he had tears in his eyes. He coughed abruptly and turned to her.

'And you will cure the sick and help the ailing? You will bring comfort to the dying and new life into the world? Is that it? You will apply your clever skills in surgery and medicine and your patients will heal and praise your name? Is that what you have in mind?'

She did not reply, except by looking directly at him for a second.

'Yes, that is it. You want to be a healer. You want only to do good.' Potter looked down at the floor between his feet. 'As did I. I was as innocent and as well-intentioned as you - what is your name?'

'Vita Carew.'

'Vita. Short for Victoria, one imagines.'

'Yes.'

'Well, Victoria. I was just like you. I wanted to do good, to help people, and so on, but I took a wrong turn, you see. Look, perhaps you would care to write this down. I should like it written down.'

He gestured towards the notebook on the bed. Vita took it up, with no idea what to expect. He nodded in approval.

'I was a foundling. Do you know what the word means?'

'I think so,' Vita said, 'you were abandoned as a child.'

'Yes. My mother left me at the gate of the Hospital for Sick Children in Great Ormond Street. It shows a certain degree of thought, I suppose. She might have put me down at any street corner, but she went to the trouble of taking me there. And she pinned my name to my shawl, I was told.'

He was speaking without looking up.

'I was sent to the nearest orphanage, and, after a year or two, a family in one of the grander houses in the city adopted me.' Potter shifted in his seat and smiled wryly. 'Oh, do not imagine that this meant happiness for the poor little orphan; it did not. I was fed. I was clothed. I was educated at the school nearby. But I never was part of the family. There were two other boys and a girl, all older. I was variously their play-thing, their slave, their project, their scapegoat, the demon-stration to others of how very charitable they were. None of them knew me or cared to know me. I was a lesser being. I slept in the attics with the servants, who also disliked me. Make sure you write this all down.'

'Yes. I am writing it,' Vita said.

'The Deakins - this was their name - were all as proud and as ignorant as human beings can be. They had no curios-ity, no longing to learn, no instinct for study, no interest in anything beyond what they could see with their own eyes in their daily lives. I was young, perhaps only five or six years old, when I perceived the significant difference between the Deakins and myself: I was possessed of the intelligence that none of them either had or valued. Asking questions was a sign of the worst behaviour, as far as they were concerned. Reading a book by choice was something unimaginable - a pure waste of time. I was scorned and ridiculed, but at school I had an odd little ally in the old woman who ran the place: Miss Brevercombe. It was she who entered me for my first scholarship. How she persuaded the Deakins, I'll never know, but somehow I was put up for the grammar school scholar-ship and won it. The Deakins were offended. They considered that I had diminished their own children by comparison, which I had. But shrewd Miss Brevercombe persuaded them that my achievement reflected only glory upon them. Their generosity had raised a genius. They must be saintly. I was a credit to them. The neighbours were wonderfully impressed. How gratifying for the Donkey-brained Deakins!

I was a scholarship boy for all the rest of my education,' he said with a long sigh. 'I could write a fat volume on the bursaries, funds and bequests available in London because at one time or other I benefitted from most of them. I am the product of charities, guilds and foundations. I am thoroughly the product of good works by the civic-minded. How proud they must all be now!'

CHAPTER 31

*P*otter smiled; a grim, dry movement under his black moustache.

'I trained in medicine at Guy's. It was gruellingly hard work, as perhaps you will discover for yourself. Ten times harder for me, whose every expense was a mighty barrier. My fellow students could pay for additional tuition, or re-sit expensive examinations; such things were out of the question for me. I lived in the grimmest of rooms. I ate the scraps left over when street markets closed. I had holes in my boots. I was always alone. I could not pay for a drink or a jovial meal with friends. No boisterous medical student befriends a poverty-stricken bookworm who cannot pay his way. Besides, I wanted nothing to do with most of them. They were golden boys for the most part, spending their family's money. The poorer ones, like me, spent their time in sweated solitary study. I did perfectly well in my academic work, but I had one great weakness as a medical man - I loathed the mess and gore. The stink of the human body and its countless revolting ailments repulsed me.'

Potter lifted his head and looked at Vita intently. 'I have wondered, occasionally, whether it is not a common thing to discover an aversion to one's chosen profession. Are there architects, for example, who suddenly find they hate building and measurements? Or fishermen who one day cannot abide the smell of fish or the roll of the sea? I imagine there are.'

'Of course, I overcame such feelings. I had aimed the entirety of my existence toward qualifying in medicine, so qualify I must, and did. I did it to spit in the eye of the Deakins family and everyone who had scorned and patronised me along the way - and there were plenty of them. Only Miss Brevercombe was proud when I qualified.'

He paused, as if allowing Vita to catch up.

'The hospital work I did in training was something I knew I should never stand for long. Sleeping in rooms like these; running about in the service of senior men, who didn't care if you learnt anything, as long as they were not troubled. I imagined that general practice - somewhere in the country - might be better. So I was junior for three very dreary years to a Dr Vinny and his doctor son in Ipswich. I was given all the worst jobs and regularly ridiculed for my book-learning and fancy scientific ideas. My patients wanted tried-and-tested remedies that were cheap and familiar. They were morbidly suspicious of anything new.

I thought I understood poverty, having scrimped and saved and scraped by throughout my education, but I learnt what hard poverty meant in Ipswich's darker corners. There were women there who couldn't remember how many children they had or how old they were because they took so much Dr Collis's. There were men who lived on fish heads and slept propped on pegs against the wall for want of enough room on the floor of the dosshouse.'

'I lived the life of a church mouse, saving every farthing, so that at the end of my indentures I should have enough to set up a practice of my own. Somewhere remote, I thought. Where I could earn a living and keep myself to myself. I could live on thin air. I was used to it.'

'It might have made for a better life if I had hitched myself to some local doctor's daughter. Most of my fellow juniors did so. There were a couple of candidates - a broad-beamed girl in Ipswich called Alison was one. We were almost engaged, but one day I heard her chatter about hats and the price of lace and realised it would simply go on and on. Unchanging. Forever. So I beat a retreat. They were dull creatures, the young women who would spend time with me. I was, I admit it, dull enough myself, but I had hopes of someone with more life about her.'

He unstoppered his hip flask and took another pull at it. It was nearly empty.

'And that,' he continued, wiping his mouth with the back of his hand, 'is how I came to Halsey. It took all my small savings and every penny of the inheritance from Miss Brevercombe, when she died, but at last I could practise medicine independent of intrusive and ignorant supervision. It was a new beginning. I left Ipswich down-at-heel, darned and downtrodden. I spent a week in Cambridge and there I reinvented myself. Elegant clothing. A decent horse - the first of my life - the nags they gave me in Ipswich would have disgraced a rag-picker. The only thing I kept unchanged was my name; my only real possession. I came to Halsey a stylish young country doctor. I set my sights on a lucrative practice, and that meant cultivating the landed gentry. If loans and credit were needed to do so, then so be it.'

Potter stood, stretched, and walked to the window. The little room was in the eaves. He looked through the falling snow as the beginning of daylight picked out the steeples and chapel towers of Cambridge.

'You are keeping up with me?' he asked.

Vita nodded.

'It was difficult to find sufficient numbers of wealthy patients to pay my debts. There are two or three large houses and a reasonable number of landed families in the area, but they are a close-knit lot with inclinations as limited as any Ipswich crossing sweeper when it comes to medicine. It was Miss Finch who intervened. She knew the families. She knew their problems, their secrets. I recruited her.'

The doctor sighed with his back still turned. His breath fogged in the chill air of the room. Vita shivered.

'Edith Finch came to work for me nearly eighteen years ago. I charged her with finding as many private patients as she could. She and I complemented one another. I have never met anyone like her. She has none of the limitations most of us labour under. She is the finest liar and the most accomplished thief you will ever meet. No conscience, you see.'

'The first special patient she found was James Lampton up at the Big House, as they call it in the village. His widowed mother was frantic. James had been sent off to Oxford as a promising youngster, but fell in with a bad crowd and returned with a degree in gambling and drunkenness. Others can indulge in a little casino-play and walk cheerfully away, win or lose, but there are a few - he was one - who become fatally enamoured with the thrill of it. They are powerless to stop. He was a promising young man - the apple of his poor Ma's eye - but in five years he had gambled away his allowance, lost his health, and acquired a substantial debt. He was pursued by creditors and had begun - and this is where the family was spurred into action - he had begun to sell land.'

'No land-owning family can stand by as a drunken heir parcels off farms and tenancies they have owned for several centuries. The Lamptons had been at the Hall since the Tudors. Unadventurous care-taking had kept the place intact and solvent, but young James was taking out mortgages left and right. It had to end. His behaviour was riotous and offensive. He was famously drunk at a party given for his younger sister and pissed in the goldfish pool in full view of the ladies. They decided he was insane and consulted mad-doctors, but they wanted nothing to do with the case. In desperation, the family turned to me.'

'At first I fancied I might reason with Lampton, which shows how little I understood the most serious kind of gambling affliction. Of course, that failed, but he agreed to consultations - to keep his mother from taking the legal action she threatened against him, I imagine. I treated him with sedatives. He was already a regular user of laudanum - he found it calming. I raised the dose, injected him. He responded well, slept better, felt less excitable and troubled. It was declared a successful treatment by the family because it kept him at home, where they could watch him. I was their last resort. They needed something to believe in.

'I was aware that the improvement was illusory. As soon as he was in a less soporific state, he began going in search of hidden brandy and talking about returning to gambling clubs to win back the money he had lost. He was convinced at all times that this remained a possibility. They always are.'

'When he was sober enough to realise the suffering he had caused, James had a conscience that tortured him. The opium kept him tranquil, but his morale deteriorated. He lost all interest in his life; wept often; lay for days on end in his bed; refusing to see anyone, to dress, to eat. In short, he lost the will to live. One day he asked me, no *begged* me - I was almost the only person he spoke to - to end his life. He told me repeatedly that he wanted to die.'

'I was shocked. I had imagined that a period of medicated tranquillity might end in a peaceful return to a form, at least, of normality. James was twenty-eight years old. His mother felt that marriage might influence him for the good, if the right young woman could be found. They were making plans for the future. They felt there was hope for the first time in several years. They were extremely grateful to me. They credited me with every improvement James had made. But they did not see him. They did not witness the bleak deterioration that was taking place upstairs in his rooms. I could not explain to them, or understand myself, why sobriety led only to thoughts of suicide. It was only the thrill of the gaming tables or the liberation of alcohol that made the world tolerable for James - and even then it was bearable only briefly.'

'Over a period of months, he begged me every time I saw him either to end his life for him or to leave enough medicine for him to do it for himself. His determination never varied. He was clear. So one day I measured out the dose he would need to put an end to it and watched him swallow it.'

'Now, Miss Carew, if I am open with you, which I wish to be, I must declare that this was not the first time I had administered a fatal dose to a patient. In general practice, inevitably, one encounters occasions when a patient's suffering is extended to an unreasonable degree. You can imagine such situations: the very slow fading of the tubercular; the gangrenous; the syphilitic - I needn't go into the details. Whatever you may be told, there isn't a medical man alive who has not hastened the end for a patient whose suffering has already extended beyond the limits of endurance. But this, I admit, was different. This was a young man with at least the theoretical possibility of a long life ahead. I helped to kill him because he begged me to.'

'James's death suited his family. But that is not the reason I hastened it. I want that noted down. I offered him the help he needed to end his life because it was a burden to *him* and he begged me to relieve him of it. I never foresaw what his death would lead to.'

CHAPTER 32

*V*ita had lost track of time. She looked up as Potter paused and was surprised to see the dawn light through the snow. Her writing hand was aching and her pencil woefully blunt. The handwriting on the page, when she looked at it, was a crazy parody of her normal script.

Potter uttered a shuddering sigh and bent his head to either side, as if his neck felt stiff, before continuing. 'I began, immediately, to receive approaches from families - some far afield - with troublesome relatives. These situations are not uncommon. Lady Celia let her friends know I was - *dependable*. They sought me out. Money was no object to these people. Edith Finch, to give her her due, had the magic touch with them. She dealt with these families in a manner they felt was both proper to their station in life, sympathetic as to their desperate difficulties, and entirely discrete. I don't know what she said to them, but I do know that over the years the practice made a fortune.'

'I do not deny that I became a little more flexible as time went by. Early on, I would only consider treating patients whose condition was as dire as James's. There were several like him - young men and women - whose actions threatened ruin and disgrace to their noble families. We always tried a period of sedation first, and in one or two cases, that led to an improvement, but it was rare. More commonly, whatever the original weakness: lasciviousness, drunkenness, gambling, religious mania, or whatever, it returned as soon as the soporifics were reduced. In such cases the families requested I hastened the end as a mercy both to the patient and to themselves. And I did so, for a suitable fee.'

'So you see, Miss Carew - Victoria - I can explain my practice. It is only taking what all medical men have done and extending that service to a slightly wider range of patients and their desperate families.'

Potter smiled and lifted the hip flask to his lips a final time. Vita was losing patience. 'You say you became more flexible, Doctor,' she said, speaking as mildly as she could manage, 'but you extended your range of 'hastening' patients to include servants as well as family members, as I understand it.'

Potter shrugged. 'Edith took the initiative there. She convinced me it was a small enough step. They were usually depraved, wanton, sick, or elderly. The behaviour of servants in a great household can be disgraceful.'

Vita wrote this down.

'I can feel your juvenile and ill-informed judgement creeping through the very air towards me, Miss Proper, Miss Science Student, Miss I-Hope-to-Qualify-in-Medicine,' Potter said. 'But if you are unlucky enough to qualify - and the odds are very much against a young woman managing any such thing, despite what they do in places like Germany - if you ever claim your MD, this is what you will find: you cannot make a decent living doctoring decent people in a decent way. That, Miss Carew, is the plain fact of the matter.'

'I shall be needing that notebook. Thank you for writing my confession. And now, I am afraid, I shall have to ask you to swallow a little medicine. I had thought to make a confession and hand myself in to the police but having explained the whole thing to you, I have changed my mind. I shall make my escape and post this, so that they can read it while I enjoy my savings in Nice or Biarritz. But you, Miss Carew, would only spoil the surprise.'

They both heard footsteps creak on the floorboards along the corridor outside. Potter froze for a moment. Vita, suddenly more alert than she had felt for several hours, eased herself forward ready to jump to her feet, but Potter turned back, and reaching into his pocket produced a small blue bottle with POISON on the label. She recognised it as an opium mixture. One of the powerful ones that Gadd specialised in.

'Now. I must ask you to swallow this medicine. You will fall asleep without pain. The door is locked. I dislike physical violence, but I'm prepared to use it if there is no alternative. Hand me the notebook first.'

'Help!' Vita shouted. It was a feeble shout. Her throat seemed dry and tight. 'Help me, somebody!' she tried again, only a little more loudly.

'Oh, come now,' Potter said. 'Such a display! You are making a show of yourself.' He took Vita by the neck of her blouse, tightening it around her throat. The repellent smell of his whisky breath was close to her face.

'Help me!' Her shout was louder now.

Potter's eyes were cold, his jaw clenched, his grip on Vita's windpipe steely as he pulled her to her feet. He forced the glass bottle against her lips. She twisted her head, but he pressed harder. Glass scraped her teeth, and tore at the inside of her mouth causing a pain that made her scream. This only made him press harder. The taste was sweet at first, syrup concealing the harshly bitter drug. Vita squirmed and spat, crying out again, fighting for a breath deep enough to slow the pulse pounding in her neck and jaw. All through the night she had comforted herself with a plan. *Two steps to the window; throw out the book; force a way to the door; if it is locked, beat on it and shout; if it is unlocked - run!*

His reflexes should have been slow, his movements clumsy, after the whisky, but still his strangling grip around her throat was unrelenting. *Two steps to the window...*

More sounds outside, louder now: a door closing, footsteps and voices. People were coming. Potter was distracted for a second. Vita gasped in a great lungful of air and flailed both arms up inside Potter's, dropping to her knees and clawing her way out of his grip. It worked, but she fell to the floor, hitting the side of her face on the chair. He kicked, aiming for her head, but making contact only with her shoulder. Here, at last, a childhood of wrestling with an older brother paid dividends. Vita wrapped both arms around Potter's ankles and held tight as he tried to kick and stamp her aside. His balance was unsteady because of the drink and the cramped space of the tiny room. He tried to reach down and grasp her head, but hit his own on the bedstead. Vita kept up a loud volley of shouts and shrieks.

'Help! Somebody help me! HELP! Mmmph!'

The last was the wordless cry of someone kicked hard in the ribs. Potter had shaken her off and snatched the notebook. He staggered for a moment, the chair in his way, and she lunged her shoulder into his waist, grabbing his jacket and throwing him backwards across the chair. The chair, already past its best years, broke and Potter fell awkwardly onto its splintered remains. Vita seized the notebook out of his hands, stepped over him and shoved the window open. This was made difficult by the snow that had accumulated on the windowsill overnight, but she wrenched the casement open and flung the notebook out. It fluttered like a shot bird in the air before diving silently down.

A crash followed, caused by the door bursting inward to reveal a large police constable with Sergeant Dunwoody close behind. Both jumped on Potter. Vita's lasting memory of the scene was a blur of blue uniforms, roars of furious outrage, and, as the dust cleared, a constable with his helmet askew, pinning a loudly protesting Potter face down on the dusty floorboards by sitting on him.

'I demand that this young woman be detained,' Potter shouted, raising his head as the constable fastened handcuffs on his wrists. 'She has imprisoned me in this room against my will and made threats against my person. She is a violent and dangerous lunatic!'

'That's quite enough of you for one night, Sir,' Dunwoody replied. 'Are you hurt, Miss?'

'I think I am only breathless,' Vita said. She pressed her handkerchief to her sore mouth. 'I must retrieve the notebook. I had to throw it out of the window. He made me write his confession.'

The sergeant raised an eyebrow. 'Did you now?' he asked Potter.

'The woman is raving. In her criminal insanity, she has held me here and while she did so, she scrawled some nonsense in a book. The ravings of a diseased mind. No court would even look at it. I repudiate it. It is a tissue of lies!'

'We'll take care of this gentleman. Why don't you see if you can find the notebook, miss?' said Dunwoody, who grew milder and more pointedly polite with every outburst from Potter.

'She is insane, a dangerous lunatic, and you allow her to wander a hospital freely? Arrest her, man!'

'This young lady's aunt is well-known to my Inspector,' the Sergeant said, as if it settled the matter. 'You sit tight there, Constable, and you, miss, run down and find that notebook of yours before the snow gets into it. And if you see Inspector Llewellyn anywhere, you might tell him Sergeant Dunwoody has captured the suspect.'

VITA HURRIED DOWN THE STAIRS, gasping as the pain in her side shot a new spasm across her ribs every time a foot hit the ground. Outside in the snow, she looked up towards the attic window she had hurled it from and tried to calculate where the notebook had fallen. There were footprints along the path to the main entrance, but the gardens in front of the hospital were virgin snow, hedges and trees picturesque in their thick white coating. Only Vita's footprints marred the white as she wandered up and down until she found what she was searching for, damp but whole and legible.

CHAPTER 33

*I*n the side room of Ward Two downstairs, Vita found Jane dozing in the chair with her cape wrapped around her.

'What of Potter? Did you see him?' Jane asked, rousing.

'I saw a lot of him. He is arrested. He held me in a room upstairs and talked all night. I took his confession.' Vita dropped wearily into the other chair.

Jane was startled. She leaned forward, looking bewildered. 'But you escaped? He confessed? To what?'

'To everything, including the murder of his patients. He gave me his whole life story. He thought he might add me to his list of hastenings at one point.'

'He threatened you? What happened to your lip?'

'He tried to make me swallow some of his special medicine. Does it look bad?' Vita yawned.

'A little bruised and swollen, but not too bad. You need a cold cloth on it.'

'Later. He also kicked me in the ribs.' Vita rubbed her aching side, leaned back in the chair and closed her eyes.

'And the side of your face?'

'I fell and hit that on a chair.'

'Vita, you have had quite a night!' Jane said.

'How is the patient?' Vita asked without opening her eyes.

Jane smiled. 'He has been awake for hours, remembering. He can now recall a little of the evening he disappeared. He was invited to dine with Dr Potter. The last thing he remembers is that the drink he was given tasted odd.'

'Potter drugged him?'

'Yes. Probably by mouth first and then by injection. Gerald spent some time on your mathematics book. He found he could answer the questions. That pleased him a great deal, because it showed his intellect was functioning, or so he said. Oh, and he has proposed marriage to me four times, at the last count.'

'Have you accepted?' Vita asked. She was not sure how seriously Jane took this.

Jane laughed, 'No. It make it a personal rule never to accept proposals of marriage from patients who are not in their right minds.'

Vita laughed too. 'A sensible rule,' she said. 'Matron would certainly approve.'

They both looked towards the patient, who was sleeping peacefully, unaware his romantic plans were being laughed about.

'I have never seriously imagined marrying,' Jane said, sounding more serious. 'Have you?'

'Imagined it?'

'Pictured yourself married in your later life.'

'I'm not sure,' Vita told her. 'I suppose I have always thought I would marry, but I have not thought when it might be, or to whom.'

'I am anti-marriage, on the whole,' Jane said.

Vita was not sure she had ever heard a young woman declare this outright before. She opened her eyes. 'Really? Why is that?'

'I favour independence.'

'You do not fear being alone - in old age, for example?'

'Not at all. There are ways to avoid that without marrying - a busy life, plenty of friends, a few dogs, and so on.'

'And children?'

'Well, children would be nice, I imagine, but a lot of responsibility. I've read a lot of anthropology. In certain parts of the world, there are societies where marriage is completely unknown.'

'Oh? What happens instead?' Vita asked, leaning back again and stretching out her legs. Her ribs were still aching from the impact of Potter's boot, but even on the hard hospital chair, sleep was beginning to overtake her.

'It varies. In some places, men and women never live together. They live in large separate houses and do different work. Children wander between the houses, happily living in both. Men and women - it is a warm climate, everyone is completely naked - both look after all the children, regardless of whose they are. Children are not seen as belonging to any one pair.'

'But how do they... how do they go about...?'

'Conceiving them?'

'Yes.'

'Well, in at least one case I read, they have picnics,' Jane said. 'Picnics in the woods. Men invite women or women invite men - any man or woman they choose - into the woods to share food, and to pass the time in other ways.'

'I see,' Vita said, now half-asleep. She was giggling drowsily. 'And is this a way of life that appeals to you, Jane? Separate houses; shared children; picnics in the woods?'

Jane lay back in her chair and laughed too. 'There may be one or two difficulties, obviously. Naked picnics are frowned upon in Cambridge, I gather.'

'They are,' Vita said. 'Wherever would one tuck one's table napkin?' She chuckled, yawned and fell asleep.

CHAPTER 34

SATURDAY, DECEMBER 24TH

*I*t was before six, and the hospital was awakening around them when the last attack occurred. Vita, Jane, and the patient were all asleep. A ward sister looked round the door into the room.

'What are you doing here? This is not allowed. You may not sleep in a patient's room. I shall have to ask you to leave,' she said, when she saw Vita and Jane.

'We saw the matron last night - and she...'

'Which matron?' the nurse demanded, crossing the room to draw back the curtains.

'The senior matron on duty last night,' Vita said.

'What was her name?'

'I do not know her name,' Vita said.

'Nor I, but she gave us permission to stay because there was an attempted assault on this patient last night,' Jane added.

'Assault? Nobody told us on the ward,' said the nurse. 'I am not satisfied that you have permission to be here.' She confronted them with her arms crossed.

'I am a nurse myself,' Jane told her.

151

'Not here at Addenbrooke's. I don't recognise you,' the other nurse said. 'Besides, this patient must be washed and prepared for breakfast. Come along now, I must insist that you leave immediately. Visiting hours are from 2 o'clock in the afternoon. You can come back then.'

Neither young woman had the strength to argue. Both were stiff from sleeping in hard chairs, and Vita was increasingly troubled by the pain in her side. They left the ward, shepherded out by the irritable ward sister, and walked up the long corridor outside, past several other wards. Nurses and doctors were coming on duty. Orderlies with trollies delivered supplies. They paused at the far end to look out of the tall arched window. The sky was beginning to clear; weak sunshine twinkled here and there on the snow. Glad to stretch their legs for a few minutes, they stood and looked out at the bustle of a new Cambridge day.

'Perhaps we no longer need to sit guard,' Vita suggested, but Jane shook her head, uncertain.

'Did Potter tell you about Miss Finch in his confession? Did he explain her role in what he did over the years?'

'He said he employed her. And that she helped to find his well-off patients.'

'Nothing more?'

'Why?'

'We don't know where she is, Vita. They are not likely to have detained her at the police station. She may still plan to come back and try to silence Gerald. If they planned everything together, she might still be following that plan.'

'On her own?'

'Why not? She might still believe they can escape, if they can only silence Gerald. She doesn't know that Potter has been caught.'

'He never mentioned Miss Finch carrying out any of the

killings herself. She referred patients; she collected the fees. There was no suggestion that she killed anyone herself.'

'But she is capable of it. You saw how insanely she was behaving on the train,' Jane said. 'They have accumulated a great deal of money. She wants it, presumably. She has worked for it for many years.'

'You make her sound like the puppet master. As if she controlled Potter.'

'She had to. He was incapable a lot of the time. She held the practice together and...'

Turning, both looked back down the long length of the busy corridor, and as they did they saw a woman's figure dart across from the staircase and slip through the double doors into Ward Two.

'Vita!' Jane said in alarm.

'Yes! It's her. It's Edith Finch,' Vita agreed.

CHAPTER 35

*J*ane outran Vita. The corridor seemed twice its earlier length as they dashed back; mouths dry and legs weak with fear. They found the side room tidy, the patient's blankets smooth, his pillows plumped. He seemed to be sleeping but something was wrong.

Jane put a hand to his cheek and then reacted sharply, throwing the blankets aside to reveal a large, dark bloodstain. Dark red blood ran with a distinct pulse from a cut on Linn's neck.

'I think it's an artery. It needs pressure,' she said, and folding a corner of the sheet into a pad, she pressed it with both hands onto the wound. 'Fetch someone, Vita, this bleeding must be stopped quickly.'

Vita ran into the main ward, a long, high-ceilinged room. Men on either side were sitting up preparing for breakfast. Their heads turned to follow her as she rushed to the nurses' table in the centre.

'The patient in the side ward needs help. Quickly. Please come quickly!'

Two nurses and a white-coated doctor looked up. Seeing

her expression, they hurried to follow. Vita stood at the door of the side room as they surrounded the bed and joined Jane in the effort to save Linn.

'Keep up the pressure. It's deep. I only hope the carotid has been missed,' she heard the doctor say.

Leaning against the wall to catch her breath and steady her racing thoughts, Vita realised she had not seen Edith Finch leave. She and Jane might have seen her if she had escaped through the main doors of the ward, but they had seen nothing.

Preceded by a rattling trolley, a porter pushed through the doors at that moment, whistling.

'You still here, Miss? My lads made fast work of them buns, my word they did!' he declared, recognising her.

'I need your help. Is there another way downstairs from this ward?' Vita asked.

'Only a fire escape at the very far end. We're not to use it except in emergencies.' He pointed towards the long ward.

'Where does it come out?'

'By the side wall on the Trumpington side.'

Vita ran. She hurled herself through the main doors of the ward and down the staircase, sending startled nurses and doctors reeling indignantly back at every turn. In the lower hall, she raced to the nearest entrance and burst through it, turning left along the snow-covered path at the front of the building. Her aching ribs made each breath painful, and she knew the chances of catching up with Miss Finch, who had crazed determination and a head start, were not good, but it was worth a try.

The fire escape was just round the corner, a skeletal wrought iron spiral addition of steps and landings towering four storeys above. Reaching it, Vita looked around. No sign of anyone. No sound. No footprints in the night's new snow.

Finch must somehow have found another way out. Vita was about to run back when she heard something. A dull ringing clang from above. She looked up and could just make out a dark shape through the grilled fire escape steps. It shifted, and the dull sound came again, along with a muted grunt of effort.

Stepping back a few paces, Vita could see the shape more clearly. It looked like a pile of blankets, but on examination, she recognised the dark grey of a nurse's uniform skirt. The figure was prone on the staircase, one foot protruding between two stairs. She must have slipped and fallen. Even from a distance, Vita could see that she was lying awkwardly, the left leg trapped and twisted beneath her body. A loud groan above confirmed that Miss Finch was in pain.

She also has a knife, Vita thought, as she climbed the stairs. *I must not forget that. Didn't Dunwoody say there were other police officers somewhere?*

The fire escape was slippery with frozen snow and icy to the touch. Climbing the treacherous stairs shook small avalanches from above. They landed on Vita's shoulders and hair, melting in freezing rivulets that ran down her face and neck.

By the time she reached the fallen figure, Vita was almost too chilled to speak, but it was clear at once that Finch could not move. Her face was grey, her lips blue with the cold and the pain from what Vita guessed must be a badly broken leg.

'Don't move,' Vita said, when she had enough breath to speak. 'I'll fetch help for you.'

'Get me up,' the woman said.

'Your leg is badly twisted. You should keep still until I can bring help.'

'What do you care? Help me up.'

'Miss Finch, your leg is broken. You cannot move. Let me fetch someone.'

'I *shall* move. Help me!'

'You cannot stand. You should be still. The doctors will know how to ease the pain before they treat your leg.'

'Shut up and help me stand!'

Even a slight movement was clearly agonising, but the fallen woman was still angry enough to raise her head and glare at Vita. The scar across one eye and cheek stood out like a pale blue lightning bolt.

'They have arrested Dr Potter,' Vita said. 'There is nothing more you can do. Just wait while I call for help.'

'You are a liar!'

'No. I saw him arrested.'

'Liar. Fool!'

'He confessed to me. He trapped me in a room upstairs and made me write his confession. He told me everything and I wrote it down.'

Edith Finch gave a series of groans as she tried again to shift her trapped leg. 'Oh, he gave you the poor orphan story, did he? The cruel adoptive family; the scholarships; the starving student?'

'Yes. And how he started mercy killing.'

'Fool! He is the biggest liar in the world. Not a word of it is true. Potter is a master liar. Now help me to stand. I am going to New York.'

Panting and holding her side, Vita stepped away and lowered herself down onto a cold metal step several feet below the prone figure of the angry woman. She fumbled in her pocket, found the silver whistle and, without a great deal of hope, blew it as hard as she could.

Fifty yards away, on Trumpington Street, the police officer patrolling the perimeter of the hospital heard the sound pierce the snowy silence and turned to run towards it. Vita saw him slip, but regain his balance as he hurried

157

through the hospital gate, but then a terrible scream rang out from above. Edith Finch had pulled her trapped leg free. She was trying to haul herself up hand over hand on the curved iron bannister, impeded both by agonising pain and the difficulty of gripping the slippery metal.

'No!' Vita cried. 'Your leg is broken. Miss Finch, you cannot stand!'

But the woman was beyond reason. Perhaps she was even beyond pain. She certainly paid no attention.

The police officer, with his greatcoat flapping, had reached the front of the hospital and was looking around. Vita blew the whistle again, and he looked up and saw her on the fire escape. 'This woman is injured. Bring help!' she shouted, leaning over the handrail to call to him. He turned and ran back towards the hospital entrance.

As she watched him leave, Vita was hit from behind - a heavy impact on her back that shoved her off balance, knocked the breath out of her lungs and forced her to her knees, clinging to the metal uprights. Confused and struggling to draw breath, her eye was caught by a dark shape that flapped and swirled. It was hard to make sense of it. Then came a loud and terrible cry, followed by the repeated metal clatter of a series of impacts below her on the steps. They rang out; a grim, distorted chime of bells, a sound Vita heard in her dreams for a long time to come. It was the grim music of an iron spiral staircase when an already unconscious body somersaults violently all the way down.

The Edith Finch they carried off later, whose blood already stained the snow, was a horribly broken thing. Dead, they said, from a fractured neck, probably before the second turn of the spiral stairs.

CHAPTER 36

CHRISTMAS EVE. SATURDAY, DECEMBER 24TH

Although both protested, Sergeant Dunwoody insisted statements could be taken later and sent both Vita and Jane back to Eden Street by cab.

Tabitha brought them hot chocolate, to which Aunt Louisa added a generous tot of medicinal brandy. She applied a cold cloth to Vita's face, but soon gave up trying make sense of their accounts of the night and sent them both to bed. 'Tell me later, Dears. It's Christmas Eve. I have a party to prepare for.'

In the time they slept, a tree was delivered and set up in the hall, together with a large bundle of mistletoe and branches of red-berried holly and ivy. Tabitha, wielding a step-ladder, decorated the hall, the dining room and the sitting room with this greenery tied up in scarlet and green ribbons, hanging it from picture rails and along the tops of bookcases and suspending it from lamps and finials. She hummed Christmas carols as she added paper chains and lanterns and was admiring her own efforts with some satisfaction when Monsieur called her back down to the kitchen.

Vita was woken after midday by delicious smells of

159

Christmas baking. Cinnamon and dried fruit, ginger, brown sugar, allspice and mace, wafted through the house from the basement kitchen. She was lying warm in her bed, slowly piecing together events of the long day and night when Jane put her head round the door. Jane was fully dressed.

'I must go, Vita. I shall call on Gerald and they will want to know where I am at the Nurse's Home, I'm back on duty tomorrow.'

'On Christmas Day?'

'Yes. The patients still need nursing. It's usually a jolly day at the hospital.'

'Oh, but please join us tonight for Christmas Eve dinner.'

'But I am not on the guest list.'

'You are, if I request it.'

'No, no.'

'Please do, Jane. I shall need an ally to help me face the determined good cheer of our neighbours. To say nothing of my brother and his friends. I find parties a trial and particularly a party so soon after everything that has happened...' Vita pulled the pillow over her head in desperation at the thought.

'I have nothing I could wear to a party,' Jane said, laughing at Vita's melodramatic display.

'Oh yes, you have!' Vita cried. She sprang out of bed and presented Jane with the large box that had been sitting unopened on her desk.

'What is this?'

'It is the kind of dress that makes me want to lock myself in a cupboard for a fortnight. The kind of dress that makes me look like a carrot stuck into a tomato. It is a red dress chosen by my dear aunt, who means only well, but cannot imagine anyone not adoring a party or the reddest of red dresses. Jane, if you borrowed it for tonight, you would be doing me the most enormous favour. It will suit your dark hair to perfection and I can wear my old familiar white party dress and feel something like my ordinary self.'

'You exaggerate,' said Jane, but as she said it, she lifted the lid of the box and glimpsed the red dress in its tissue paper. 'Oh, my word! That truly is a *red* red!'

'Yes. And even from across the room I can see how well it suits you, you know it does.'

Jane laughed, 'It's lovely. And we are more or less the same size.'

'Good. So you will come tonight then?'

'Only if your aunt agrees.'

'She agrees!'

'Alright. If she really does, please thank her and say I accept.'

CHAPTER 37

$\mathcal{T}$he party began with champagne and the ceremonial lighting of the Christmas tree candles.

This was an exciting annual moment for Aunt Louisa. Each year the tiny candles in their silver holders were fixed among the branches of the tree and each year she said a prayer to the gods of household safety as she lit them, because the flames that looked so pretty also risked setting it alight. The fire bucket had been needed on one or two occasions in the past. They had never so far caused a mighty conflagration, reducing the house to a heap of smoking ashes, but every Christmas Eve as she lit the taper Louisa pictured the possibility.

The candles having been admired (and safely extinguished) and a Merry Christmas toast drunk by all, they moved to the dining room for the feast to begin.

Vita was next to Dr Goodman on one side and her brother's friend and employer, Aloysius Derbyshire, the fencing instructor, on the other. The face of one guest nearby seemed puzzlingly familiar. It was only after the oysters that she realised he must be Professor McGuinness - he of the immense beard and angry goat eyes whose portrait her aunt had just completed.

'How are things at the gymnasium over Christmas, Mr Derbyshire?' Vita asked him.

'They are splendid, Miss Carew. Quite splendid. We have a new class - callisthenics for ladies - hugely popular - the boxing is expanding rapidly, and of course the fencing just grows and grows. And then there are the classes in Eastern combat, people adore them. One is quite rushed off one's feet! And how is undergraduate life?'

'I am rushed off my feet too, mainly for fear of being left behind in maths and physics.'

'Maths? You find mathematics difficult?' Derbyshire asked, squeezing lemon over an oyster.

'Terribly.'

'Really?'

'I never had proper schooling, you see.'

'Oh, dear me. That would put you at a disadvantage.' Derbyshire swallowed his oyster, closed his eyes briefly in enjoyment, and picked up another. 'But surely in Cambridge it should be easy enough to find someone to offer tuition? There are several mathematicians among my clientele at the gymnasium, for example.'

'But would they be willing to teach someone at a low level? Would they have the patience?'

'It would not suit them all, I suppose. One such is here tonight. Mr Denver, Barney - Barnabus - Denver. He is there, sitting beside your brother.'

There was indeed a young man beside Edward. He was examining an oyster as if he feared it might bite him.

'And Mr Denver is a mathematician?'

'He is. Top man, so they say. Extremely clever. Rather shy. Comes to me for fencing lessons on a Thursday.'

'I am prepared to beg him for help on bended knee, but I am short on funds to pay him,' Vita said.

'His handwriting is very poor,' Derbyshire said. 'I know, because he sent a terrible scrawl the other day to re-arrange a lesson. You might trade some tidy writing, or something of that sort.'

'Thank you, Mr Derbyshire. I shall propose exactly that to him as soon as dinner is over.'

Derbyshire looked pleased.

Vita did not feel up to eating oysters herself. Catching Mr Denver's eye across the table, she moved hers quickly onto Aloysius Derbyshire's plate. Denver, looking relieved, immediately did the same, shifting his oysters onto Edward's. For the rest of the meal she and Denver caught each other's glances and when it was time for pudding and the lights were darkened for its arrival, flamed in brandy, they were already wordless across-the-table allies. This meant that when Monsieur entered with his Christmas dessert, they were in a good position to share the joke silently.

At first sight the spectacular construction he lifted onto the table was an odd, prickly Christmas tree.

Guests looked impressed, but also confused.

With a showman's flourish, Monsieur plucked the holly from the towering dessert, revealing a three-foot pyramid of plum-sized Christmas puddings. The diners were just wondering what magic could hold this gravity-defying dessert together, when he stepped back, doused it with brandy from a copper pan, and set the whole thing alight.

All gazed as sizzling blue flames danced about the great pyramid of puddings, filling the room with a delicious smell of brandy, caramelising sugar and roasting fruit. Then, before anyone could tell how he did it, the tower was doused and disassembled and everyone had been served their own little pudding set in a creamy moat of brandy sauce.

As his finishing touch, Monsieur produced two small flags: a French *Tricolore* and a British Union Jack, and stuck one into each side of the pudding he set before the hostess.

For a moment Louisa Brocklehurst's eyes narrowed, and her lips parted, ready, Vita imagined, to utter some blistering remark. The rest of the company looked on, expectant, but then their hostess gave one of her most charming smiles.

'Ah, Monsieur Picard,' she said, 'Émile! You are always the innovator! Ladies and gentlemen, a toast to Monsieur Picard and to Anglo-French harmony.'

'Monsieur Picard!' the whole company agreed, raising their glasses.

'*Vive la France*!' some called.

The chef bowed and backed in the most stately manner out of the room.

The puddings tasted superb, and many guests declared them a great improvement on the usual Christmas pudding. Monsieur had even hidden a silver coin in one.

After dinner, all assembled in the sitting room for carols around the piano. Mrs Goodman played, her husband supplied a sonorous bass, and everyone joined in with their favourites.

Jane, it turned out, had a fine soprano voice, and sang a short duet with Edward, displaying both her singing and the red dress at their very best. Edward seemed particularly impressed.

While the audience called for *encores*, Vita crept out and found Mr Denver alone in the empty dining room, reading. He started and looked guilty.

'Oh, please excuse me. I was distracted by this volume I

found on the hall stand. It is anti-social to read at parties, I know, everyone says so, but this is such a dear old friend. It takes me straight back to my school days.'

He held up Vita's copy of *Pure Mathematics*.

'It is mine. The book, I mean. I'm Vita and you, I know, are Barnabus Denver.'

'Yes, I am. You do not care for oysters, either, Vita, I noticed.'

'No. I was at a dinner once where...' Vita shuddered and left the sentence unfinished.

'Ah,' he said. 'It is more the look of them I find discouraging.'

'Mr Denver, Barnabus, I urgently need a mathematics tutor. I am in my first year at Newton college and I am being agitated, made miserable and generally defeated by every page of *Pure Mathematics*. I feel like running fast in the opposite direction whenever I see that volume you are so fond of. I am a capable enough person. I know I must square up, intellectually, to many challenges, but when it comes to maths...'

'Alright,' Denver said.

'And then, for the last few days, there has been this dreadful incident at the hospital. There was a man with no memory and I became involved, when really I should have been... Did you say *alright*?'

'Yes. I will tutor you, if you think it might help. I may not be good at explaining, but I'm willing to try.'

'You will?'

'Yes.'

'And your fee?'

'I did not think of asking a fee.'

'Oh, but I must pay for your time. You must have some

reward. I'm told your handwriting is, perhaps - well, that it might not be - perfectly, well, perfect.'

'Indeed, it is notoriously poor,' he said.

'I could write things for you, perhaps, now and then, in exchange.'

'Send me a note at King's tomorrow, and we shall make arrangements. I have never taught anyone before. I make no promises as to my ability to do so, but we agree on oysters, so mathematics should be easy enough.'

'Could you start by explaining the square root of 1095.61?'

'Now?'

'Yes, please. Unless you would prefer to join in the singing.'

'I would *much* prefer the square root of 1095.61,' he said. 'Now, in a square root of this kind, a certain amount of guess-work is required at the beginning…'

THEY DID maths until they were caught and called back into the room to take part in Dr Goodman's experiment. He had brought with him to the party his mysterious invention. When pulled from its bag, it turned out to be a set of wooden pieces hinged and joined with pulleys. Nobody could make anything of it, but he laid it on the carpet and explained that it was a life-sized model of a human arm and a shoulder.

'This is my patent device for training medical students in replacing a dislocated shoulder. It is a skilful procedure, painful for the patient and difficult to practise. My model here allows a student or a first aid trainee to apply the right pressure in just the right way, so as to ease the ball joint - *here* -

back into its socket - *here* - without causing a real patient any pain.'

'Good heavens!' Aunt Louisa said.

'How very ingenious!' someone more medically inclined declared.

'The ropes and rubber strips you see on either side, *here…*' Goodman continued, warming to his subject and evidently planning to explain every detail and intricacy of the complex device.

'… Shall we just allow guests to try it out, my dear?' his wife suggested.

Dr Goodman accordingly demonstrated his device by sitting on the floor, placing a foot in the wooden 'armpit', grasping the roughly shaped wooden hand and pulling strongly back. When the right tension was achieved, the model's wooden shoulder re-located itself into the correct position, causing a small bell to ring.

Although there was more music and dancing later, and the party continued well into the small hours of Christmas morning, it was undoubtedly the Goodman Shoulder Relocator that made the most memorable impression on many of the guests. All the men had to try it, including Professor McGuinness, whose face turned an alarming shade of purple when he hauled on the wooden arm. The ladies, too, took their turns. Jane struggled to pull hard enough, but kept going until she succeeded. But Vita found she had the knack of it almost straight away.

'We all know who to turn to if we dislocate a shoulder!' Dr Goodman remarked. 'I shall call upon you, Vita, to demonstrate it when the heads of medical schools from all around the country beat a path to my door. As I confidently expect, they soon will.'

'I hope they will, too,' his wife remarked to Aunt Louisa as they watched the Shoulder Relocator put through its paces from the sofa. 'But I shall not hold my breath, since they did not beat paths to our door for his Jaw Strengthener or his Toe Flexor which followed similar principles.'

CHAPTER 38

'*H*ow do you think it will it end for Potter?'

'He will hang, I imagine,' Dr Goodman said. He was collecting up his Shoulder Relocator. It was well after midnight. Most guests had left.

'He is insane, I suppose.' Vita pushed the wooden hand into the Shoulder Relocator's bag.

'A man like Potter thinks himself superhuman, far too clever to be convicted by ordinary people in an ordinary court of law. He made himself into a sort of god, by deciding who should live and who should die.' Goodman stood, shaking the bag to settle the wooden arm into position. 'It must be a shock to realise his powers are not as almighty as he believed.'

'Is that sort of delusion common among doctors, do you think?' Vita asked.

Goodman stopped what he was doing and considered this question, stroking his beard. 'I am not trained in psychiatry,' he said. 'It would be interesting to put that to someone who is. It might be the other way round; that characters who already over-estimate their own powers are drawn to medicine. Most would soon be cut down to size, but a few, like Potter, might sustain their delusion. There are maniacs in every profession, no doubt.'

'I cannot tell how much of his confession was true. Miss Finch told me it was all lies,' Vita said. 'All that about the deprived childhood and his struggles as a student.'

'Some of it, I'm told by colleagues, is true,' Goodman said. 'He truly was a scholarship candidate and an orphan, but liars often use the basis of truth. There was something about Potter and Finch together that caused lies to flourish. The pair of them constructed their own world of deceit there in Halsey.' He pulled the strings that tightened the neck of the bag.

'How was Dr Linn when you saw him last?'

'Recovering well. He can be discharged in a day or two. Whether he will want to go back to practicing medicine in Halsey is another matter.'

'Will they really hang Potter?'

'If he is found guilty, yes. But I have my doubts.'

'You doubt a court would find him guilty?'

'No. I doubt he would ever submit to such a thing.'

'How could he not?'

'Whatever else we think of him, we must admit that he is a clever man. My guess would be that he will bring about some quicker exit for himself. He excels at hastening death, after all.'

CHAPTER 39

THURSDAY, DECEMBER 29TH

*J*n the steamy kitchen of the great house, Cook tasted the gravy warming on the range and threw in a pinch of salt. The servants' dinner was nearly ready.

'Blimey! It says here Potter's done himself in,' Litcombe remarked. He was sitting by the window, reading the newspaper.

'I thought he was locked up,' Cook said.

'He was. *The prisoner was discovered in his cell at Cambridge Police Station. He is believed to have taken his own life.* Found him yesterday, it says here.'

'Bless my soul!' Cook said. She wiped the blade of her carving knife and squared up to a steaming leg of mutton. 'Don't they keep an eye on them? Don't they search their pockets and such like when they lock them up?'

'You'd have thought so,' Litcombe said. 'Somebody must have helped him out.'

Cook pushed the carving fork well into the meat and sliced towards the bone. 'How do you mean?'

'I mean someone took him what he needed. A little bottle of his own medicine, I shouldn't wonder.'

'Who'd want to do that?'

Litcombe set his newspaper down and looked across the kitchen. 'Her Ladyship was out for a long time the day before yesterday.'

Cook stopped mid-cut and stared at him.

He raised an eyebrow. 'Easily long enough to get to the police station and back. And to buy some special medicine.'

'You can't just buy poison from a pharmacy these days,' she said.

'Potter's medicines come from Gadd's. I've read the labels. Have you ever seen Gadd's shop?'

'Not I,' Cook said, still vigorously slicing mutton.

'Well, I have. Gadd's not the type to ask questions. Specially not if a grand lady walks in and asks for one of Dr Potter's special mixtures. Helping Dr Potter on his way might suit Lady Celia quite nicely, if you think about it.'

Cook stopped slicing and pointed her knife at him across the kitchen. 'Don't you dare say a thing like that out loud in my kitchen, Harry Litcombe!'

The butler shrugged. 'I said nothing.'

'Mind you keep it that way.' She laid the mutton slices on the serving dish. 'Now, get this along to the table before it goes cold. And just you remember who pays your wages, my lad. And mine.'

ALSO BY FRAN SMITH

Poison at Pemberton Hall

A dazzling diva. A glittering society dinner. A servant with a terrible grudge.

Bookish, bespectacled Vita Carew longs to be left to her scientific studies. But she cannot avoid the event of the season, a gala at Pemberton Hall. This glamorous concert and sumptuous dinner will mark the Pemberton household's return to society after a run of misfortune.

But disaster strikes as soon as the seafood is served. Vita can only offer first aid as elegant guests fall suddenly ill on all sides. Worse still, she suspects a death has been covered up to avoid interrupting the carefully planned soirée.

Vita must probe dark secrets behind the country house's elegant facade to work out who is to blame. But can she do so in time to prevent the poisoner from striking again?

If you enjoy a stylish mystery with your Downton Abbey, dip into Poison at Pemberton Hall today.

A Thin Sharp Blade

Shortlisted for the Crime Writer's Association Debut Dagger Award 2019

Snubbed by professors and male students alike, Vita Carew longs to study science but can only borrow books and work alone.

When a popular boxer dies and her brother collapses after an exhibition match, she spots a connection the experts have missed. The very professor who brushed her dreams aside is the one she must convince.

Can Vita, with the help of a secret society of women students, an energetic swordsman and a strange lady photographer, convince the experts she is right and prove what really killed the boxer?

And how will the glamorous widow react?

A splendid bit of gothic-tinged fun.

A witty mystery with a feisty heroine and irresistible period touches.

Slip A Thin Sharp Blade into your handbag today.

Available for pre-order soon:

The Killing at Crowswood

REVIEWS

Independent writers depend on word of mouth for their publicity, so if you enjoyed Dr Potter's Private Practice, leaving a rating or a quick review is a great way to help other readers discover it too.

These shortcuts make it easy:

US

UK

Thank you!

ACKNOWLEDGMENTS

My dear team of checkers, supporters and helpers were much needed while I was finishing Dr Potter. I am grateful to them for reading, editing, proofreading and being full of strong opinions, especially about what should happen to Potter and Edith Finch at the end.

I hope you enjoyed the result.

The character of the matron at Addenbrooke's Hospital was inspired by Alice Fisher who trained under Florence Nightingale and started the school of nursing in Cambridge in 1876. She went on to work at Philadelphia General Hospital, where she is remembered as a great influence for the good. She died in 1888 aged only 49 years and is buried in Philadelphia, where there used to be an annual pilgrimage of nurses to her grave.

She must have been the most extraordinary and admirable woman.

Fran Smith
September 2021

Oh, and one more thing…Edward Atkins *Pure Mathematics* is a real book. In case anyone is beating their brains over the maths problem that gives Vita so much trouble, (page 85 Question 7: *Extract the square root of 1095.61, and find to three places of decimals the value of 4/√5 - 1.*) I'm glad to say that Mr Atkins provides the answers too. They are 33.1 and 3.236.

Many of you had easily worked that out, of course.

ABOUT THE AUTHOR

Fran Smith lives in the flat fens north of Cambridge, England and writes looking out at a completely horizontal view. At the moment she spends a lot of time inventing picturesque ways of killing Edwardians.

The Vita Carew series has led her into researching the struggle women endured in order to study science and medicine in the early part of the 20th century. The amazingly determined and impressive pioneer women who led the way are an endless source of inspiration.

You can sign up for newsletter updates at the website or find her on Facebook or email fran@fransmithwriting.co.uk